My Only Real Friend is the Easter Bunny at the Mall

Christina Bagni

Winnipeg, Canada

Developmental editor: A.K. Adler
Proofreader: Margaret Larson

Published April 2023 by Deep Hearts YA, an imprint of Deep Desires Press and Story Perfect Inc.

Deep Hearts YA
PO Box 51053 Tyndall Park
Winnipeg, Manitoba R2X 3B0
Canada

Visit deepheartsya.com for more great reads.

For S.G.D.

My Only Real Friend is the Easter Bunny at the Mall

One

*Bet You Didn't Think It Would End
with Me Getting Arrested*

"Impaired concentration, insomnia, loss of interest, fatigue, significant weight loss," Dad told you, counting off on his stubby fingers. That's five out of the top seven symptoms of low to moderate depression, a.k.a. the reasons he shuttled me off to a therapist.

I knew parents didn't usually sit in on sessions, but he'd been overprotective like this since Mom overdosed, so I wasn't too surprised. I sat on the overstuffed couch beside him and tried to avoid speaking for as long as possible.

I didn't even look you in the eye for like, ten minutes. You were there for this, of course, so you probably remember that—but I'm writing this because I want to tell you everything that really happened, because who knows if I'll ever get to speak to you again—and "everything" includes my first therapy session. When I *did* look up at you, I thought you were pretty, for one, and kind of young, but obviously trying to look serious, with your glasses and everything. Your hair fell like two vertical window blinds on either side of your face. I wondered, when I met you, if you had ever done anything crazy with your hair, like dying it pink or shaving half of it off. Have you? I can't really picture you doing anything crazy, at all.

Eventually, you asked Dad to leave so we could have privacy.

Dad's undereyes did that awful creasing thing that happens when he's worried, which is pretty often. I first noticed it during new-student orientation a few years back. His hand gripped my shoulders in the auditorium, and when I saw his undereyes I got stressed out without even knowing why.

"You tell me right away if you get bullied, okay?" he'd said.

He didn't have to be so worried. I had never gotten bullied before—not really—and even in the ridiculously white suburb we had to move to, I wasn't bullied. I made friends with Claire and Nora pretty quickly and didn't have any problems. But Dad grew up Black in Boston in the seventies, and I guess he figured that even the lighter skin and good hair Mom gave me might not be enough to save me here. It's useless trying to get him to calm down about anything danger-related.

Whatever, anyway.

"Maureen," you said after he left, and I corrected you right away with, "Mo, please."

You smiled. I liked that you didn't say sorry.

"Mo." You sat forward and leaned your elbows on your crossed knees. "Did you ask to come here?"

I shook my head, smiling. You saw right through him. It was awesome.

"Do you *want* to be here?"

I thought about it. I wasn't sure, which is why it took me a while to answer (see? I told you—I want to tell you everything. I didn't tell you a lot during our first few sessions. Not stuff like that. I want to fix that, now). I had been feeling sad, but that wasn't exactly anything new. It was only new that Dad noticed. I nodded, trying so hard to look like I was taking it seriously—because I was.

"I'm just not sure if I need it," I admitted. "I mean...I don't want to die. I haven't been like, *beaten* or anything. I don't feel like I...you know."

I wanted to say, *deserve to be here.*

"Your dad said your mom's been gone for five years."

I nodded again.

"No one ever gets over the death of a parent. Not really. It must have been hard."

"Yeah." My voice came out creakier than I meant it to.

"Do you think that might be what has been affecting your sleep?"

Maybe. I mean, it's not like Mom...it's not like I've forgotten about her. It's just that I'm...not *over* it, but, Jesus, it's been five years. I can't still be worked up over it every day.

"I don't know. I try to sleep, but I can't, so I throw on a movie or play a game."

"Online video games?"

I'll be honest, it was hard to hold in my laughter here. I think a little chuckle escaped, but I didn't mean for it to. It wasn't even funny, really, it was just that such a professional, blonde lady with glasses—a real *doctor*—trying to use the right lingo…"online video games." You said it as if it clarified something, as if—I flattened my lips.

"Yeah. Or whatever else."

"Why do you let those things distract you?"

Um, okay, bitch.

Sorry, sorry. That's what I thought, though. I'm trying to be honest.

"I don't know. I just do."

So, after we talked for a little longer, you decided that in order to fix my insomnia, I needed *another* distraction. That didn't really make sense to me, but you were the professional, so whatever—and, to be fair, you meant something *productive*, something after school but before bed that wasn't just "online video games." But, yeah. A distraction from my distractions.

First, you suggested doing a sport, and I laughed, and you laughed with me, which was nice.

"Not your thing?"

I told you the story of my one attempt at softball. I didn't tell you the Mom part of the story. You laughed.

"Okay. Maybe music, or art? Theater?"

I'm about as talented as a brick.

"What about just a job?"

I frowned a little, just for a second. *I guess I could get a job.* A short one. I was a camp counselor in the summer, and in September I'd be going to college, but maybe something before the camps start up would be good. Having spending money would be nice.

And like you said—maybe it would *distract* me.

Therapy wasn't so bad. I didn't have to cry on a couch

or anything, like I thought I would have to. At the end of the hour, you told my dad that we talked about getting a job, and I figured that would be it. Dad works as a mall cop at the Carlindale Mall. He knows all the stores that are hiring. He'd actually been trying to get me to work at the mall since I turned sixteen, so I accepted my fate as a clothes-folder and actually felt okay.

Anyway, that's how I ended up working for the Easter Bunny.

Two

The Bunny Boss

I'm sorry if you don't usually get letters. I didn't even set this up like a real letter, with a date and a salutation and all that. It's just that after all the…well, you probably saw the news. After all the craziness that happened at the mall, I wanted to tell you everything, like I said. And it's always been easier for me to write out my thoughts than to say them out loud. I have more time to think, this way, and I don't get nervous or mess things up. Besides, what else am I supposed to do in an empty jail cell? So anyway, I hope you're okay with reading letters.

I should also probably tell you that I'm writing all this on the day before Easter, and if I rush in places, it's because I don't know when they're going to move me from the holding cell. I'm just going to start writing, and I'm not going to stop until either they make me or I'm done, and I think that will probably make me feel a little better. And also explain to you everything that's actually been going on. And distract me from having to pee, because I really don't want to use the toilet in front of other people.

Okay. So anyway, after you suggested I get a job, Dad got me right into an interview to work on the Easter Bunny photo set. He told me at dinner that there was an opening to work with the Easter Bunny and I laughed, thinking it was a joke. It was entirely *not* a joke.

Early in the morning, Dad led me through the white marble side-entrance of the mall and stopped in the security office for something. I'd been in the security office a thousand times. I used to throw my backpack in an unused locker while I wandered around the mall after school, but now that I have a car, I didn't need it anymore. It was kind of nostalgic to be back in the boring blue office with the worn-down carpet and waiting-room chairs nailed to the floor. The walls were all glass. Dad's desk was behind another wall of glass, a separate office because he was the head of security. He needed some papers, apparently, and once he had them, he led me across the nearly empty hallway, then through a giant gray door marked PRIVATE.

Only personnel were allowed back in the service hallways, even though the doors were always unlocked. They weren't anything special, just unfinished hallways behind the stores. Out front it was polished marble and up-kept cypress trees, but back here it was raw, unfinished oak boards and stained cement floors. Dad told me not to touch the walls or I'd get splinters. I knew that already.

Claire, John, Nora and I used to sneak back here when we played hide and seek in the mall. They were technically off-limits because we were supposed to stay in plain sight of the main hallways, but no one really followed that rule anyway. I once played on my phone in a Macy's fitting room for two hours before they found me. The service hallways were awesome shortcuts, so if you thought you might get caught you could duck in one and pop out halfway across the building.

But I'd only been in the service *hallways* before, never behind any of the padlocked doors—though I had jiggled several handles. I'd always figured they all led into the back rooms of various stores, but apparently three doors down from the entrance across from security was Max's office.

Max was the head of the Easter set (yeah, they call it a "set," like it's a film or something), and he looked just as unfinished and disheveled as his quote-unquote *office*. It was dimly lit by one fluorescent bar and an out-of-place golden floor lamp, the walls were cement with splotches of primer here and there, and behind the desk littered with paper and an ancient desktop computer was a giant red sofa chair covered in files, a bunch of cardboard candy canes and other props, and a tote bucket full of white, sparkly garland. Off to the left was a mirror and a clothing rack sparsely populated by four fuzzy, red-and-white Santa costumes and two full-length bunny suits, one with a blue vest, the other bright pink, head to toe.

Dad knocked on the doorframe as he pushed into the room. Max was on the phone, pacing behind the desk and a moth-eaten, black leather chair.

"Yeah. Yeah, yeah. Look, Artie, I'll call you back later, arright?" he shoved his phone in his back pocket, then ran his other hand through Greaser-like hair.

"Hey. You must be Mo."

I hesitated, then Dad nudged my back with his elbow. I took a few steps, reached over the desk, and shook his hand. He nearly pumped my elbow out of its socket. The cuffs of his too-bright teal jacket bounced around his skinny, hairy wrist.

"I'm Max," he said. He had really big teeth. I smiled and said something lame. "How's it goin'," or something like that.

Max then shook Dad's hand. "Gerald," he said warmly. "Thank you so much. You know we're always scrambling this time of year."

"Hopefully Mo is a good fit."

I don't know if you've ever gone to an interview set up by your parents, but it felt stupid—like a formality. When I "interviewed" to attend the summer camp I'm now a counselor at in fifth grade, Mom told me not to worry. She said they basically just wanted to make sure I wasn't going to do anything crazy or stupid, like kill someone during archery class. I treated this interview the same way. After all—he said he was *scrambling*.

Even if he wasn't scrambling, it wasn't like Max *wasn't* going to hire me. He and Dad were obviously buddies. When Dad stepped outside and Max, instead of sitting in the comfy office chair, cleared his messenger bag off of an iron chair just so he could straddle it backward like the cool kid in detention I knew I had this in the bag. I had an inkling Max would hire the chair itself if it could run the register.

He gestured toward a metallic stool and I perched on it, hooking the wide heels of my boots into the rungs. I kept my hands on the rim of the stool for balance.

"Alright, Mo," he said, drumming his thumb on the

top of the chair back. "Why don't you tell me why you'd like to work for the Easter set?"

Ah, damn. An open-ended question. I've always been shit at those. I'm alright at thinking on my feet, but *talking* on my feet is difficult. I trip over my words and start fumbling.

Probably shouldn't mention that to the dude hiring me for customer service.

I kept myself from shrugging, only barely, and instead went with, "I like Easter. And I like helping people."

Not bad. It would be pretty hard for me to accidentally reveal that either of those were lies. Max sort of frowned, but it was a frown of approval. He nodded.

"Mmhm. Yeah, okay. And why are you *really* here? I'll tell ya." He pointed at me. I was still processing the fact that he didn't accept my answer. I couldn't very well tell him I was only here because my therapist told me to get a job, could I? "You need the money. Or, considering your dad, you *want* the money."

"No, I—"

"Can't be here for the prestige, or a career step, or because it's cool or fun. You don't have a criminal record or a tattoo that keeps you from a normal job. You're not a college kid looking for seasonal work, and you're not an addict—"

My stomach clenched hard. "I just—"

"You just want the money. That's okay. We're all on the same page here. I just want to be clear—working here won't be some kind of magical wonderland like you thought this place was when you were a kid, you know that, right? It is going to be a real *job*, arright? You can't just call in sick ten minutes before your shift, and it's not—"

He went on like that for a *while*.

I knew already that the job would kind of suck. It's *retail*. But I wasn't in it for the money. He was wrong about that. I was only getting a job because you told me to get a job (and I was only getting *this* job because it's the one my dad got me), but I wasn't about to tell Max about my therapist. He already knew about my budding career's sad reliance on my dad.

I let him rant at me. Then his phone rang, and he groaned out his nose and said he had to take it, so he did. Didn't leave the room, though.

I glanced around the tiny, misshapen office while he talked on the phone. Behind the big Santa props and the clothing rack, I noticed a line of cardboard boxes filled with green sweatshirts and red vests, untidily folded and dusty. My own phone buzzed—probably just this game I play trying to get me to open the app again—but I didn't check it just then. It didn't seem professional to do so, even with Max himself on the phone.

Max eventually hung up and looked over his shoulder to where I was staring.

"That stuff's for Santa," he told me. "The bunny stuff is already down there."

"You run the Santa thing, too?"

"Bunny, Santa, and anything else they end up inventing. St. Paddy's Day leprechaun is my next bet. Or something...pumpkin-related." He shuffled some papers on his desk, flipping some over to check the back. "You have a resume, Mo?"

Ha. "No."

"Ever work? Volunteer?"

I scanned my memory. Suddenly it seemed like I had never done a single thing in my entire life.

"I'm a camp counselor in the summer," I offered.

"Okay, not bad. How about sports?" Max tried. "Things you do for fun?"

That was ironic, I thought, because you asked pretty much the same thing, and your solution was to get a job. And here I was, trying to get a job, and he asks me the same question you did. I guess the real solution was to already be doing something else.

But come on, Mo, what do we do for fun? What's something we can tell him—something that's legal?

"I ride my bike," I found myself saying. "And watch classic movies. And I sew."

"Sew?"

"I make clothes. And blankets, pillows. Dolls. And I embroider."

And I sound like I'm about seventy.

He twisted his mouth up, but was hard to read. I couldn't really tell how I was doing. How bad would it look if I couldn't even get a job my dad handed to me?

"Well, that may come in handy. The suits are getting old, especially that pink one," Max said finally, nodding at the clothing rack. "Which some idiot shrank in the dryer last year." He leaned back in his chair. It squeaked. Sweat glistened in his sunken cheeks. "Well, this is a great job for the basically inexperienced. It's short, pretty easy, and most people don't hate it. I'm a little hesitant to hire the kids of people who work at the mall. Last year—you know the Changs?" I shook my head. "They run that kids' clothing store up by the food court?" I smiled nervously, shook my head again. "Yeah, well. They pawned their son off on me for Christmas and the kid smoked up in my office every break he got. When he actually *came* to work. But you look like you've got some work ethic, and your dad's one of the only people in this mall with a head on his shoulders, so I think we've got us a deal."

He reached out his hand. I hesitated, a bit in shock, but then I shook it. His palm was rough, like the bottom of my feet.

"Congrats. Set opens tomorrow morning. Can you start tomorrow, after you get out of school?"

I guess so. "I don't have to wear the bunny suit, right?"

"Nope. Not unless someone decides it's rabbit season and we need a replacement."

That was the first time I really smiled. Max was morbid. I liked that.

Three

Dad bought me dinner on the way home to celebrate. He seemed really happy for me, which felt a little disingenuous. I still didn't feel like I did anything but what I was told to do, but I wasn't about to pass up his suggested celebratory Chinese food. We ate on the couch right out of the take-out containers and watched an old Kurosawa film. I managed to finish like a fifth of my Dinner Combo B before it made me want to throw up and I had to put the rest in the fridge.

"So, you nervous?" Dad asked when the credits started. "First day on the job tomorrow. Excited?"

I so didn't want to talk about it.

"Yeah," I said, standing slowly, stretching. "I am. I think I'm going to get some sleep."

"Okay, bud. Good luck tomorrow. Maybe I'll swing by!" I guess I made a face, or maybe didn't make a face fast enough, because he started laughing too hard. "Just kidding! Just kidding. I won't be throwing off your groove."

"Oh," I said. "Okay, cool."

"Just one thing," he said. "We've seen a couple of…sketchy characters hanging out in the parking lot. You know—covered in tattoos, the whole thing. Promise me you'll be safe there after dark, and if you ever feel weird about someone, call me. Okay?"

I didn't think anything of that, at the time. Dad was always warning me of sketchy characters and razorblades in my Halloween candy and the statistics of getting crushed by vending machines and whatever else was scratching his anxious itch of the day.

"Okay. I will."

"Okay. Good. Goodnight," he said, quiet now. "Hope you *are* excited? About the job?"

"Yeah, totally."

"Good…good."

I rolled my eyes when I knew he couldn't see me. I don't know why he would expect me to be excited about a lame job *he* got me.

Truthfully, I didn't know why I didn't feel much about the job, one way or another. I never really knew *why* I felt anything.

The mall had one huge main hallway with three branches cross-sectioning from its center. The Easter set was in this wide-open space in the dead center of the mall, where there were usually just sofas or pop-up stands or a car for sale. I always used to wonder how they got those cars in there, until Dad showed me the loading docks, which explained a lot.

The set was egg-shaped. I mean, the carpet was egg-shaped, the archway at the end of a long velvet-roped line was egg-shaped, even the cash register desk was egg-shaped. And it was all just a surreal, candy-coated, pastel hellscape, with everything soft blue or soft green or soft yellow or soft white. It gave me a toothache. The bunny, who I hadn't officially met yet, sat on a throne that was, yup, egg-shaped. It was a gigantic colored egg that was half-cracked into the shape of a chair, and he sat on a yellow cushion that I guess was supposed to be the yolk. Kind of morbid. Beside him was a giant basket full of those crappy dollar-store chocolate eggs that had a seam right in the chocolate where the two sides were fused together in the factory. A bunch of umbrella-shaped lights directed the flash of the camera right at him. As I got closer to the set, he pulled a kid onto his knee and smiled for a photo. The flash nearly blinded me.

I showed up at three my first day and Max started by giving me a pastel pink vest with a name tag that was, of course, egg-shaped. Then he trained me on the cash register in about thirty seconds. All the prices of the various packages and frames were taped on the table by the keyboard, so it was just a matter of plugging in the code and running the credit cards.

Max took over the camera while I rang up the next few families. I was nervous, at first, but I got pretty good at it pretty quickly. One guy even tipped me. Or, us. Apparently, we were all supposed to split the tips at the end of the day. Seems weird, in retrospect, that we even accepted tips, but we did. I was making twelve dollars an hour, so I wasn't going to complain.

It was March 16th and Easter was still a month away. Four weeks. So it wasn't too busy yet, which was good.

Once the line was clear, Max slapped me on the shoulder blade. My vest slipped around a little with the force.

"Great job, Mo! You're a natural."

Cool. I'm finally "a natural" at something and it's running the register for a giant bunny.

"Thanks," I said with a smirk, my eyes locked on the yellow-pink-blue, egg-patterned carpet.

"Isn't she, Billy?"

The six-foot, soulless bunny gave a loose-fisted thumbs-up.

He was in the nicer costume of the two I had seen in Max's office the day before. Instead of the matted, bright-pink suit, his was thick and white, with long ears lined with soft pink felt. The same felt was on his nose, finger pads, and belly, but most of his belly was covered by an *Alice in Wonderland* white-rabbit-esque blue suit jacket and yellow ribbon bowtie. He also had thin, gold-rimmed glasses without lenses, behind which blue eyes were printed on mesh.

I gave a thumbs-up back, and the bunny put his hands over his mouth and shook like he was laughing. Yikes.

"Let's get you trained on camera, too," Max said. "While no one's here."

He put his hands on my shoulder blades and careened me toward the expensive-looking camera station Max himself had been running since I'd gotten to set.

Getting trained on camera was also ridiculously easy. It was locked in place. All I had to do was look in the lens (Max called it a "viewfinder"), get the kid to smile, and press the button.

Twelve dollars an hour for this. Shit. In four hours I'd have almost fifty bucks. That's what, four movies? Two movies with snacks?

I always knew school was lying. I mean, we're only in school to train up to get a job, right? Well, I got a job. And it's not a job I needed school training for, so...

Well, whatever. I shouldn't really be complaining.

Some more customers came, and I took their pictures. The first one was pretty nerve-wracking, imagining the photo I took hanging on someone's fridge for years to come, but by the fifth or sixth I'd gotten it down.

Then a baby came.

I mean, obviously the baby didn't have a say in the matter, but it did *not* want to be there. It made that abundantly clear.

The second its mother got out of frame, it burst into red-faced screams. I cooed and waved my hands and tried to get the baby to smile, to look at me, to stop crying, nothing. Billy kind of bounced it around, then got the baby to look up at the bunny face, which obviously did *not* help. I turned back to the parents with a smile they didn't return, then looked over to Max, who was busy selling a bigger package to the last customer. My pits were sweating so hard I was sure they'd start dripping soon. I bolted over to Max.

"Um, this baby won't stop crying."

"Did you try the doll?"

I glanced back to the camera, mystified. Sure enough, there was a little stuffed baby chicken hanging from the camera stand by a blue string. *Why the hell didn't Max tell me this was here?* I rushed over, grabbed the doll off the stand (poorly made, holes in the stitching), and took a few steps forward. I went to give it to the baby. Obviously, this was stupid in hindsight, but I was panicking and the mom looked wicked impatient.

Then the bunny—Billy—held up a paw like "Stop," and jiggled his hand up and down like he was shaking keys.

Holy shit. Duh.

I shuffled back to the camera. I could feel my cheeks heating up. I shook the doll above the camera and looked through the lens, my right thumb hovering on the button, ready to attack at the slightest approximation of a smile. The bunny pointed at the doll, his other fingers awkwardly half-curled (not a ton of mobility in there), trying to get the baby to follow his gaze. The baby paused for just a half second, and I seized the opportunity. Click, flash, and it started crying again.

"Got it," I muttered, and the mom ran in to collect her kid. She grabbed a chocolate egg, even though I was sure the kid was too small for it.

"Sorry," I added as she sped by me again on her way to Max. She acted like she didn't even hear me. Whatever, okay, fine. Fuck off.

While the next kid was getting settled, I figured out how to see old photos on the camera and found the one I just took of the baby. I mean, the baby wasn't smiling, but it had on a curious little face, its mouth in a cute "O." That was probably the best face I could have possibly gotten out of it. If it wasn't so pink from crying, it'd make a good poster advertisement.

But okay, whatever, lady.

Four

The Man Behind the Bunny Mask

I was only a couple days away from turning eighteen, so I could work a lot of hours, but they still didn't want me to "close" on my own, which is work lingo for "put everything away at night." That's what Max said at first, anyway. He also said "we" a lot, so I figured I wouldn't be the only employee (besides the bunny, obviously), but for the first few days, I was.

I think I formally met Billy three days in. It was definitely a Wednesday, which I knew because I was coming in to see you after work, which was only really important because it meant I was leaving work early to get to you on time.

I was working the register my whole shift that day. Max showed me how to ring people out, too, and how to frame the photos. There were a bunch of tiny little egg frames that people usually bought to put the wallet-sizes in. They were pretty small, pretty cute. They could fit right in my vest pocket.

You know. Hypothetically.

There were some bigger things, too, that would be harder to fit in a vest pocket, and some weirder ones—like snow globes, which were super annoying to put together. But I did it, when people bought them.

Max said I should take my break when Billy does now, instead of going separately, so he didn't have to take over both roles of camera and cash when the rushes started coming in. Today, since I was leaving early, I could escort Billy to the break room—which was actually just Max's office, where I did the interview, escort him back to set, then leave right after.

The bunny apparently needed an escort because they were afraid of potentially getting sued should the bunny do something so un-bunny-like it scars some little kid for life. Like taking off the head, or smoking in the bunny suit— which, funny enough, were the first things Billy did when he and I finally got to Max's office.

He pulled off the paws one after the other, gripped that heavy head by the neck, and yanked it off his head so violently it might have scarred even me. He was turned away from me, but I saw him scratch the back of his shaved head.

He took a deep, satisfying breath, a tattoo crumpling in the folds of his neck.

"God, it's sweaty in there."

I laughed a little, not wanting to start a conversation. I was kind of in a rush. I mean, not really, but I wanted to run down to the food court and grab an iced coffee before I had to bring Billy back. I could have grabbed one afterward, but I wanted enough time to drink it before therapy so you wouldn't think I wasn't taking therapy seriously.

So anyway, Billy. There was a tattoo on the back of his neck, and when he looked down, I could see it was of a woman in a fancy ballgown and masquerade mask, just chillin' on a loveseat, throwing a handful of playing cards up in the air and laughing. It was kind of neat. He was digging around his folded-up jacket, and I was getting my wallet out, but then he stood up straight, a pack of cigarettes and a lighter in his hand.

"You mind?"

I didn't answer, but not because I minded—because I'd seen his face, for the first time. And it was covered with tattoos.

It was really well done. He had two devil horns on his forehead, a big capital H on his chin, and dark shadowing around his eyes and on his nose, temples, and cheeks to make him look like a skull. He reminded me of Day of the Dead parades.

"No, I don't mind," I mumbled.

He nodded, popped one in his mouth, and plopped down in Max's office chair. I told myself to stop staring, but I couldn't. They looked awesome. Of course, I could hear my grandmother's voice—*Why would somebody do that to themselves?*—and Dad's warning—*You see someone like that, you cross the street and you walk the other way*—but I couldn't help it. How often do you see a gangster in an Easter Bunny suit?

"I'm not in a gang," Billy said suddenly, like he'd read my mind. I looked away. "So, you don't have to be afraid of me."

"I'm not afraid of you. I think your tattoos look cool." I tried to make the pitch of my voice low enough to be taken seriously. I still kind of sounded like a little kid sometimes.

Billy smirked, snapped his thumb against the plastic yellow lighter and breathed the flame into his cigarette. "Well, glad someone does. They're actually why I'm here. The few grand I get from being a bunny is going right into tattoo removal."

Wait—he's getting paid *thousands?!*

"It costs that much?" I asked instead.

You're probably wondering why I'm writing out this entire, boring conversation. I guess I don't really know, either. I guess I just want to remember him as much as I can.

He breathed out a smooth line of smoke. "Mm. Cheaper to cover up, but. That kind of misses the point."

I smiled. He smiled.

"Are you getting rid of all of them?"

"Nah, nah. Just the ones on my face. I like a lot of my other ones—not that you can see any right now. I've got a mermaid here—" He ran a hand up his side, then across his chest. "Some planets, and a copy of my grandmother's rosary. I like them. I've gotten some dumb ones covered up—this real stupid one of Daffy Duck smoking a blunt I got turned into a pirate ship, I like that. But the face ones... they can go."

"Hm. Well, I see why," I said. "But they look cool to me."

"Just tired of everyone being afraid of me," he said. "If those moms knew I looked like this, I can guarantee you they wouldn't plop their kids on my lap."

He seemed nice. Maybe mid-thirties, though it was hard to gauge with the tattoos. I shuffled a little, took a half-step toward the stool I had sat on during my interview, then chickened out and just kind of sank into one hip.

"Can you spare one?"

He didn't make a big deal of it, just held out the pack. I considered trying to tap it the way they do on TV, where just one cigarette shimmies out, but I figured I'd just manage to shake all the cigarettes on the floor if I even attempted to look cool, so I just pulled one loose. I glanced surreptitiously at the one between his lips. Okay, the brown part goes *in* your mouth. I could never remember which way was right. He handed me his yellow lighter.

Okay, so I was a newbie at the whole nicotine thing, but I'd smoked weed, so I knew how to ease into it. I held the smoke in my mouth, not letting it into my throat. It came out too dark on the exhale. He knew I didn't really smoke it. I hit it again, letting a little down into my lungs. It didn't seem to do much.

"So, hey," he said. "Can this stay between us? Usually, when Max takes me down, I get changed and rush out to smoke outside, then change again and by then, my break's over. But it's such a pain in the ass. Max doesn't want me to smoke in here, so—"

"As long as you don't say I was the one who stunk up his office, I won't tell him," I said.

"Deal."

He held out his hand and I shook it. Much warmer (and drier) than Max's. He had tattoos on his hand, too, but I didn't get a good look.

"But you know he's going to find out, right?" I said. "When the whole room smells like cigarettes?"

"Eh. I don't think he *really* cares, he just wants plausible deniability. So he can tell *his* boss that it wasn't him."

Made sense. I smoked a little more. It was kind of going out already—I had lit it like an idiot—so I hit it with the lighter again.

"So, where you running off to? Big Wednesday-night party?"

"Ha. No—"

"Sports?"

What is it with everyone asking me about all the sports I don't do?

"Therapy," I said.

I kind of wanted to shock him. Make him uncomfortable. I don't know why. I think I mostly just wanted to seem damaged, or hardcore. Like, *yeah, I've been through some dark shit. I'm in* therapy. *And I'm so confident in myself I don't mind admitting it to basically a stranger.*

He nodded, leaned back in Max's chair. His bunny body looked pantsless when Billy crossed his ankle over his knee. He considered me with a brow furrowed in approval.

"You know, that's great," he said, pointing his cigarette at me like a mobster. "I love how you younger kids are destigmatizing mental health issues."

I snorted, and his eyes widened in earnestness.

"Seriously! I wouldn't be comfortable just *telling* somebody that I went to therapy. Now, maybe. Not ten years ago, when *I* was supposed to be in high school."

"Oh. Thanks."

I smoked faster. I didn't feel like talking about generational differences of mental health beliefs with a man in a bunny suit. But then I started coughing, because the universe hates me.

"You okay?"

"Yeah, yeah." I coughed. "Wrong pipe."

Genius.

"It was good to—" *cough* "—finally meet you. Hey, I'm gonna grab an iced coffee; can I get you one? I have a gift card, so I don't mind."

"Nah, I'm good, thanks. Too much caffeine this late and I can't sleep, you know? But nice to meet you, too!"

He smiled brightly. I tried to match it, coughed, and ducked out of the room.

I still had like half a cigarette. I held it close in my hand in the service hallway, hoping my hardest it wouldn't set off some alarm—or worse, somehow notify my dad directly. There were no cameras back here. There was no trash, either. I twisted it on the floor to put it out, which left a dark, ashy mark on the floor, then peered out the door into the mall. The security office was manned by the secretary. No Dad in sight.

I used to hate that he was always doing rounds around the mall. Now I'm thankful he can't stay in one place too long. I would probably die if he watched me work all day, and I would *definitely* die if he saw me with a cigarette.

That said, I still had to be sneaky. So many people knew me in this place. I tossed the crushed-out cigarette in a trash can in front of MakeAlive Cosmetics and worked through the irrational fear that it would somehow start a fire while I bought my stupid coffee.

I avoided the left side of the food court because this kid

who goes to my high school works at the pizza place. The lady at the coffee counter was named Mae, and she knew my name and order. I'd gone there probably a thousand times since we moved here. I actually liked a different coffee now, but when she sees me coming up the escalator, she likes to start making my coffee already as a sort of inside joke. And I think it's cute, because she's like a little grandma, so I don't mind drinking the extra sugar I used to like four years ago.

I exhaled out the side of my mouth as I paid. I didn't want her to know that I smoked a cigarette. I felt like it would disappoint her. And, also, she might tell my dad.

Mae checked me out and I rushed back, escorted the bunny back to set, did the same evasive maneuvers past my dad's office as I did to the pizza place, and drove off to therapy with the windows down, hoping to blow the smell away. I really didn't want you asking me if I smoked.

You did.

Five

That Time I Told You I Smoke Weed

"So, I got a job, like you suggested." I sunk into the poofy sofa. It's really too poofy. I feel like my dad even saying this, but you need one of those little back pillows. Lumbar support, you know?

You were still settling in, sitting in your office chair, pulling out the right notebook. "Oh yeah?"

"Yeah. I take the photos at the Easter Bunny place at the mall."

Your face lit up a little, but then you froze, like you weren't sure how to react.

"You can laugh," I said, and smiled at myself. "It's kind of funny."

You shook your head, kindly. "It sounds like fun. More fun than most minimum wage jobs."

"Yeah."

"Is it?"

"It's alright." I shrugged, and you waited, so I added, "I mean, I just started."

"Gotcha. Well, what do your friends think?"

"I haven't really told them about it yet."

You perked up, shifted a bit. "Why don't you tell me about your friends?"

"Like what?"

"Like, what do you do with them?"

"Mostly just hang out."

"Where?"

"Mostly at one of our houses. Or in the woods, behind Claire's."

"Claire is one of your friends?"

"Yeah."

"Can you tell me about her?"

"Um...she's in the orchestra."

Pause. "Anything else?"

"I dunno."

"Aw, come on, you can't tell me *anything* else?"

Isn't this supposed to be about *me?* "She's cool. We used to hang out more before she started dating this guy John, but now he's around all the time. He's probably in the woods behind Claire's right now."

"I see." You made a note. I tried to guess what you were writing. "And...what do you do back there? In the woods?"

"I don't know. Just like, hang out."

"Talking?"

I sighed out, "Yeah, I guess." It wasn't a frustrated sigh, or I tried not to make it sound that way, but I *was* a little annoyed at having to define the term "hang out," and I was getting impatient waiting for you to get to the point and start healing my depression. I didn't get what any of this had to do with anything, honestly.

"So, you just hang out in the woods, doing nothing, and...talking."

"Pretty much."

"Talking about what?"

"Nothing, really. Nothing important."

You had your elbows leaning on your crossed knees, and you kind of looked like a pretzel. Your face was kind of twisted up, too, examining me a little. I tried to keep from blushing, but thinking about it only makes it come on faster.

"You know I can't tell your dad if you smoke weed or drink, right?"

I was surprised you said "smoke weed" and not "do pot" like most adults, especially since you didn't seem to understand the phrase "hang out."

"Okay."

"It's called doctor-patient confidentiality. I can't tell anyone anything you tell me—unless I think you're going to hurt yourself or someone else. Then I have to call the police. But anything else, it's just between us. Even illegal things, like drugs and underage drinking. Did you know that?"

"No." You waited. I glanced around at your diploma, the Georgia O'Keefe painting, some trinkets on your desk. That table with a box of tissues only an arm's length away. Eventually I added, "Okay, so yeah. We go into Claire's treehouse to smoke weed."

I really didn't know why this was important.

"Why?"

"Why?"

You nodded. I inspected the succulent on the bookcase against the wall. It was growing right out of the clay pot, trying to escape. "I don't know. The same reason people drink. It's fun." That sounded lame. "Relaxing."

"Do you ever hang out and not smoke?"

"I mean yeah, I'm not addicted."

"I didn't say you were."

"I just smoke with my friends sometimes, that's all." Jesus. Relax.

"Okay. So you hang out, sometimes you smoke. And you talk about nothing. Do you ever talk about real-life stuff?"

"Like what?"

"Each other's families, your futures, problems you're having, stuff like that?"

"Not a lot."

"Do you ever?"

"Sometimes."

"With who?"

Nora. Or at least I used to.

Nora was so cool. She played electric bass in a jazz band with the best saxophone player in the school, Katie. Katie *carried* the marching band, but Nora played Katie under the table. Nora wore a plaid flannel around her waist, like a grungy model, and always flung a slender, gorgeous hand on your forearm when she laughed at your jokes. She was very touchy, actually. She always plucked fallen eyelashes off my cheeks and had me blow them off her finger to make a wish. She liked to thread her arm through mine and walk like *Little Women* through the woods, laughing as we got out of step.

And she was there for me, after Mom died. And she just *got* me, a lot of the time, and I got her, too. Most of the time.

But Nora hated her parents, and that was one thing I just couldn't get.

About a month before, Claire, John (Claire's boyfriend), Nora, and I were in Claire's treehouse. Yeah, it was February, but do you remember that really warm week, when it hit fifty? We were all in lighter layers, excited to be able to smoke outside again instead of having to find some sketchy place to park John's car. Claire was rolling a joint on this little kiddie table, because she always does it best out of the four of us. John was playing with these plastic, dollar-store darts and complaining about how he paid Claire's older brother like seventy-five dollars for a bong we never use. Then Claire was telling him that it wasn't our fault he's bad with money and besides, if he cleaned it once in a while, we would use it, and John was asking her how he was supposed to clean it without someone's parents seeing. Then John went off about his cousins in Seattle who apparently told their parents they smoke, and about how afterward, their parents took out a bowl and a grinder from the seventies and smoked with them.

I was playing Blocki on my phone, this game that was popular two years ago that I just never stopped playing. But I was listening, distantly, and I said, "That sounds so impossible."

Then Nora said, "What, the weed part or the 'loving parents' part?"

I looked up from my phone to glance at her. She was sitting on the floor and messing with something. I can't remember what. A Rubik's cube or a thing of play dough, one of Claire's childhood toys. I stared at her for a minute, but she didn't look up from the toy, so I went back to Blocki.

"The *weed* part," I said, choosing to ignore what she was getting at. "I can't really imagine *parents* smoking with their kids."

"That's the problem with this fucked state," John said. "We gotta get the fuck to Seattle." Then he missed a dart throw spectacularly—it lodged itself in the wall and a chip of damp wood flew out to land by Claire's toes. She laughed, which annoyed me for some reason.

"I can't really imagine *parents*," Nora said, ignoring John and copying my rhythm to make a point, and it was honestly so bullshit because John and I both tried to keep the subject on weed and she had to try to change it twice just so she could vaguely bitch about her parents like she always does, which was fucked up because her parents were both alive and both always came to her jazz shows and orchestra concerts, which I knew because so did Claire and John and I. And she was so supported and loved by everyone around her, and so talented and pretty and everyone wanted to be with her and she *still* complained, *still* twisted the conversation so she'd have the *chance* to complain, and I just *hated* her right then for not knowing how good she had it. Or for knowing and not caring, or whatever she was doing.

So I dropped my phone to my lap and said, "Oh, fuck *off*, Nora."

Everyone looked at me in surprise. To be fair, Nora's comment didn't exactly warrant that reaction, but you have to understand, it wasn't just that moment, it was a build-up of all her other moments. All the other times I had to listen to her bitch about a life that was way better than mine. And I don't know, in the moment, it felt justified.

It was quiet for a sec. Claire lifted the joint to her mouth and licked it to seal it, trying to act like she was ignoring me.

"Um, what?" Nora said, chuckling once like she wasn't sure if I was joking. I probably still could have played it off like I was, but I didn't.

"Your parents are fine. They may not smoke with you but they're good parents."

She put down the toy and pulled her spread-out legs in so they were crossed. Then she pulled one ankle up to rest on her other knee like she was doing yoga, which for some reason pissed me off even more.

"You like, don't know what my parents are like," Nora said, shaking her head but not looking up from the floor.

"Oh my god, they're alive. Right? They're both alive, so yeah, you can fuck off with your bitching."

The initial hot fire of my anger was already tapering off, but I couldn't just stop there. I should have, maybe.

"Um, just because my parents are alive doesn't mean they're good parents."

"Guys," John said. "Can we just—"

"No," I said, keeping my eyes on Nora. "No, you know what? I don't care if they're terrible parents. They're *alive*, so you can just shut the fuck up. And you know what else? When you came out to *your* parents, fake as it was, they accepted you, didn't they? 'Bad parents,' please."

She stared at me in silence. And it was awful, because she was my friend, but at that moment I wanted nothing more in the world than to see her cry. I wanted to *make* her cry. But she didn't cry. She just tightened the flannel around her waist, grabbed her black backpack with all those enamel pins, and climbed down the ladder with one hand. We heard her land with a thud and walk with her heavy boots across the frosty grass. She left the toy on the floor so I went over to pick it up and put it back in its little plastic bin, under the bench. Then I sat on the bench, pulled out my phone, and quickly lost my Blocki game. I felt three times my size, an awkward, gangly mess, face burning red. John and Claire were talking quietly about homework, a classic fake conversation.

"I mean, you guys think I'm right, right?" I asked after a minute. We all heard Nora's car start, then drive away no faster than usual.

"Sure. I mean, your mom is dead, so." Claire gave me this weird, unimpressed look.

"Wait," John said to Claire. "Is Nora...gay? I thought..."

Claire shook her head. "You weren't there for that."

He dropped it, which was probably the right choice.

Then Claire lit up the joint and, after a hit, passed it to John, who hit it twice then silently passed it to me. I sucked in too much on purpose, held it, let a little out slow, then coughed out the rest.

"Jeez," I said with a smile. "So coughy."

Usually, Claire made fun of me for coughing, but this time she just nodded.

"Happens, sometimes," she muttered.

Shit. I fought to stop coughing. Couldn't. Eventually did, my eyes watering. I felt like an ass.

But I couldn't say any of this to you, then.

So, "My friend Nora," I told you eventually. "But we haven't been talking lately."

"Why not?"

"I guess we're both busy. Homework and stuff."

A classic fake excuse.

You changed subjects and kept asking questions about my job and whatever until our time was up. On my way out of your office I fished around my jacket for my car keys and found a lighter. Billy's yellow lighter. Oops.

Been a long time since I'd stolen something by accident.

Six

Victimless Crime

I couldn't decide what to do with Billy's lighter. Surely, he had more than just the one. And if he didn't, well, they were like, a dollar. He could just go buy one. But maybe he was poor. He'd have to be, to be working the Easter Bunny gig—what non-poor, non-retired person is able to work a low-wage, seasonal job?—but he'd also have to have enough money to afford getting those tattoos. Unless they were done by a gang.

Or in prison. I mean, he had to have been in one or the other, right?

Whatever. Mostly, I didn't want him to think I was a thief.

I thought all this while in my bedroom, looking through my closet of stolen things. Not everything in my closet was stolen, just most of it. Like most of my bras, for instance, a bunch of my sewing stuff, my earrings, my makeup, and a bunch of stupid knickknacks—like a set of these stand-up Batman figurines. Oh, and a bunch of books, too! Those were hard. Damn. But not everything. I have a shelf of all the dolls I make, for instance—but then again, they're made of a lot of stolen fabric, so.

I figured I couldn't really judge Billy if he was in a gang, since I was a serial shoplifter.

By the way, before you judge me, I only ever shoplifted from mega-corporations because, you know. Fuck capitalism. It's a victimless crime. I don't think any gang is "victimless," especially now that weed is legal. So, maybe our sins aren't very comparable after all.

Billy did straight up say, "I'm not in a gang," and I was inclined to believe him—but he didn't say "I was never in a gang." So he might have been, I figured, in the past. And so what, I guess, if he used to be in a gang. He seemed nice now. And he was trying to get the tattoos *off*, so he was obviously over it.

I put his lighter next to the Batman figurines, then tried putting it next to these little Japanese erasers shaped like cats, then in my jar of stolen pencils.

Then I put it back in my jacket pocket. I only like to do *victimless* crimes. Dude's already scrounging for tattoo removal. Might as well not cost him another dollar for no reason.

Then I went back to work finding a place to display the four-inch, egg-shaped photo frame I snagged from work. I had slipped it into my vest pocket that afternoon when I was on the register, right under Max's nose.

Mom would be so proud.

Seven

Gotcha

The next day at work, I waited all day for a good opportunity, but not once was there a moment when Max wasn't looking *and* there wasn't a kid around who'd ask why the Easter Bunny needs a lighter. So, when I headed out (because Max never had me stay all the way to close), I slipped it into Billy's jacket pocket with a corner ripped out of my math notebook, saying: "Sorry. Accidentally stole this from you." I figured he'd know who it was from, so I didn't bother signing. There was a tiny hole in the jacket, its green canvas blackened and burned through on the cuff. Maybe from a cigarette. I ran my thumb over it. Maybe not? I could fix it, if he—

"Hey," someone said from the door, just as I had my hands all over Billy's jacket. I whirled around, jacket in hand, because *that* didn't look suspicious. It was Billy, the bunny head tucked under his arm like a basketball, its dead eyes smiling at the ceiling.

"Oh, hey—"

"You need something in my jacket?"

He raised an eyebrow, and the skull tattoo of his face morphed. It looked like the bunny head was the skin, and his body the bones beneath. That gave me the creeps more than his menacing voice.

"Oh, no." I fumbled, dug in his pocket, and held up the lighter too fast, breaking my attempt at nonchalance. "I took this by accident yesterday. I was just putting it in your pocket. I didn't know you'd be back so soon."

He waited a full two seconds after I finished to reply. He reminded me of you, when he did that. I felt my chest and armpits sweating under all my layers. Billy came up and took the lighter. He clicked it on with one swipe of his thumb, then let it go out. He seemed relaxed, but something in the air had me on edge.

"You took this by accident?" He took his jacket from me next, slowly.

"Yeah."

"Did you take that little picture frame by accident, too?"

There it is. I felt my face flush. No point in arguing; he'd obviously seen me slip the picture frame into my vest pocket yesterday. I licked my lips and picked up my bag to go. To run if I had to.

Billy chuckled a little, unconvincingly, like when Dad laughs before telling me "I don't think so" when I try to go over Claire's too late at night.

"I'm not mad, dude," Billy said. "Doesn't affect me. But you know the stores do inventory every night, right? Max knows a frame was stolen, he mentioned it after close. You're just lucky you did it on a day when he ran cash for half of it. He can't blame you."

"He couldn't have known *I* took it."

Billy laughed again, too loud. He waddled past me and

flumped down at Max's desk, began to work off the bunny shoe covers.

"Yeah, he wouldn't have assumed you took it, but you were on *cash*, dude. You'd be to blame for not watching the merch close enough. He was just *also* on cash, so he can't be sure if it was your fault or his."

I rolled my eyes. "You can't blame the person on cash for someone else being good at stealing."

"Alright, man, whatever. Look, like I said, I don't care if you took the frame. It's a weird thing to steal, to be honest, but, you do you."

"Cool." I turned to go, one hundred percent done with this conversation.

Then, out of nowhere, Max burst the door open with his foot, carrying the expensive camera and the lock box of all the cash and receipts. Standing in the doorway, he tossed his head to get strands of greasy hair out of his eyes.

"Hey, which one of you two assholes are smoking in my office?"

Ha. I kind of wanted to out Billy, but he obviously had something on me, now, too. I felt like I finally understood that "mutually assured destruction" we were supposed to be studying in history class.

Max rolled his eyes when neither of us answered. "Well, whoever it is, I don't really care, but if this one's cop dad finds out, I'm throwing both of you under the bus."

He held out the camera to me expectantly, and I took it, not sure what else to do. "Lock that up in the bottom drawer, will ya? I gotta go deposit—" he raised the lock box, then glanced down at it and adjusted his stance. "Hey, you wouldn't know anything about a wallet-sized egg frame, would you?"

Oh, goddammit. "The one with the chick on top?"

"No, just the egg ones. Did one break or something? We're missing one in inventory."

I ran some crazy calculations in my head, trying to figure out if he was trying to trap me or if he really didn't know at all. "Nah," I finally said. "I dunno."

"Huh. Okay." His expression was unreadable. "Thanks. I don't mean to be on your asses," he said, now addressing both of us. "We've just had some pretty bad employees the past couple years. Some addicts, some…" he glanced at me, and I think he remembered about my mom, because he dropped his harsh voice a little. "You know? I think you're both cool, but I…" he waved his arms around. "…you gotta…you know? Okay, see ya."

And he was gone, the heavy clinking of the lock box disappearing down the service hallway. I gave the camera to Billy to lock up then fumbled with my jacket, waiting until Max was nearly out of earshot before turning to go again, hoping I could keep my tears of embarrassment from falling until I got in my car.

"Wait—Mo."

I dropped my head back to stare at the ceiling and turned slowly, mad at Billy's condescension and mortified at being called out and ready to run and quit and never look back. He was leaning down to deal with the camera but poked his head up above the desk to talk to me.

"Be careful. You're a senior in high school, right?"

"Yeah."

"You eighteen?"

"Almost." I put a bit more oomph behind this one, trying to walk the line between letting him know I was annoyed without annoying him myself. "My birthday is tomorrow, actually."

"Really?"

"Yeah."

He smiled. "Happy birthday."

"…thanks."

His smile faded a little. "Just so you know, everything changes at eighteen. They won't just call your parents if you get caught. They'll call the police."

What, over a four-dollar picture frame? Please. Just because he was in a gang or whatever doesn't mean he knows a thing about what I do. It's entirely not a big deal.

But I didn't tell him that. I just said, "Okay. I'll be careful."

But seriously. My dad *is* the police, so what's the fucking difference?

Eight

Elise

Alright, so, I was just frustrated at being caught. I know there's a difference between someone calling my dad and someone calling the police. I even know there's a difference between my dad and "real" police, though he acts like there's not.

Big one: he doesn't have a gun. Well, he, personally, has a gun, locked up in a safe in the basement. I used to know the code, since there was other stuff (like some of Mom's jewelry she somehow never pawned) in there too, but after he put me in therapy, he changed the combination. Anyway, he doesn't carry a gun on the job. I don't think he's allowed to. He used to carry one when he was a university cop, but those days are long gone.

Another big difference between my dad and a real cop: he doesn't work in a police station. His office in the mall had less real estate than the mall's Dunkin' Donuts.

Even the mall security office would be easy to steal from. I haven't (yet), but it's possible. I've been in there enough, waiting for dad to get off shift to drive me home. Now that I have a car, I don't go in much, but it would be a breeze.

There's no merchandise there, obviously, but all the

mall cops have their things in these lockers. Dad used to let me use one, back before I could drive, to throw my school stuff in before he got off work. Head cop perks. It was nice to wander around the mall without my books weighing me down.

Easier to shoplift that way.

Now that locker belongs to a new cop who's only a few years older than me. Unlike Dad's safe in the basement, I doubt the combo has changed on that locker. I could totally take the new guy's walkie talkie or doughnut or whatever.

But just because a lift is possible doesn't mean it's a good idea. Mom could probably manage it, but I'm nowhere near as good as she was. Mom liked nabbing makeup, since it was expensive and sold well, and, as far as I know, she never got caught by Dad. Which was great, because that meant he didn't have any reason to suspect I was doing the same.

In retrospect, she hid a lot from Dad. I don't know how he put up with it all and still came out the other side in love with her.

Mom and I would go into a store and she'd lift a hundred dollars of eyeliner and lipstick without me even noticing. She was training me in her ways before she passed, when I was only thirteen. That's why I'm so good at bras, by the way. I was just beginning to need them when Mom started training me. We walked into Walmart and Mom directed me to the back corner, two hands on my shoulders. She whispered hot in my ear: "Do this right, and you'll never pay for a bra in your life."

And I haven't. Yet. So far.

Of course, I only got to keep some of the bras we stole. Most of them, my mom took and sold.

The day after Billy confronted me over the picture frame, it was my eighteenth birthday. Dad had gotten me a nice pair of earrings in the morning—too nice for me to wear without worrying about losing them. Claire and John and a few other friends met up with me in school to wish me a happy birthday. Claire invited me to come over to her place Saturday after work to celebrate. I said I would, so long as Nora wouldn't be there. Claire sighed, but agreed.

Before my shift, I took a detour down to the mall's Pandora's Box to steal a bra. A present to myself. I've hit it only a few times, because they're kind of ritzy. Hitting a high-end store is something of a challenge—at least more than at Walmart, where they practically expect you to steal something. I actually don't even wear most of the bras I've taken from there. I have them in a shoebox in my closet, all black lace and red bows. I just take them because I can, and because fuck Pandora's Box.

So, here's how my mom taught me. You go in, grab a bunch of bras on hangers and one not on a hanger. Sandwich the one not on a hanger between two on hangers. Tell the person managing the changing room that you have one fewer item than you do (if there isn't a person managing the changing room, you're golden). In the changing room, put the bra on over (or under) your normal bra after removing any tags, then get out. Buy a lipstick from up front to sway suspicion, if you feel like you need to.

So, I went in. Red, black, purple, hot pink. Lingerie on perfect models. Lace and ribbon. Price tag more than I made in a day—and those were the ones on sale. It made me sick.

Billy could claim it "wasn't" a victimless crime all he wanted. These retail people weren't paid on commission, I was pretty sure. I certainly wasn't. They got paid like I did, by the hour. And no one could claim it was *their* fault if one bra of thousands went missing, or was miscounted. Plus, it couldn't cost fifty dollars to make a bra, so it's not like I was even hurting the company too bad. The Pandora's Box conglomerate wouldn't even notice, what, five dollars of bra material missing from stock? No one would notice. No one would get hurt, except me if I got caught, which I never did.

You know, I just realized I'm probably the only biracial kid in the country whose white parent made them more wary of the police than their Black parent did.

Anyway, I grabbed a few pricey ones, black, all of them. Best not to be memorable. Then I picked up a soft cotton one from the shelf without a hanger and sandwiched it in. All going to plan.

I headed toward the changing room. A girl with dreadlocks that looked to have been dyed blonde once a couple months ago was sorting bras by size behind the podium.

"Um, hi," I said. She turned around, tucking a fat lock behind her ear. She had on thick-rimmed, ice-blue glasses. I was kind of surprised Pandora's Box let her in the door, never mind gave her a job. She looked so…*cool.*

"Hey," she said with a warm, peachy smile. "Trying them on? Or do you need a fitting?"

"Just trying them on."

"How many?"

"Six."

She didn't check. She fingered through the number tabs then gave me one with a big 6 and walked me back into a pastel-pink changing room with a chintzy, rhinestone lamp.

"Let me know if you need anything!"

She gave me a smile and, my god, she was pretty. So pretty I had to catch my breath after I closed the door. I held my pile of black bras to my chest, looked my reflection in the eye, and laughed into my hand. Wow. Dreadlocks, kiddie glasses, the grace to work at Pandora's Box, and so, so pretty. Pretty and cool.

I chastised myself playfully while hanging up the bras. What kind of a feminist was I, anyway? Surely, she's funny, smart, adventurous. I bet she goes on all the big roller coasters.

Maybe. But at the moment, all I knew about her was that she was pretty, and I was *mad* attracted to her.

So, I don't know if her kindness and smarts were already rubbing off on me or what, but I decided to stop stealing right then and there, and I haven't shoplifted once since!

Ha. Nope. I wish, because that would have saved me a lot of bullshit later on.

Instead, I did this:

I tried on some of the decoy bras for fun and danced for myself in front of the mirror, pretending I was the kind of New York City rich girl who could wear expensive bras to penthouse parties like it was nothing. Then I put on my normal bra, then the one I planned on stealing (after checking all over for tags and tracker chips) over top of it. Then I pulled on my shirt and walked out.

"Back already?" the pretty attendant said, a mark of concern in her brows. She pushed back the unbuttoned flaps of her uniform blazer to put her hands on her hips and—oh, okay—she was wearing suspenders.

This might actually be a go.

Okay, so that might sound like a stereotype but…to be completely honest, I'd never seen a straight girl wear suspenders. So, I was really just using statistics to my advantage.

"Just got the wrong size, I guess."

"Oh! Well, I can help with that." She disappeared behind the podium and came back up with a tape measure. "Have you been measured recently? We just started selling half-cup and quarter-cup sizes, so we've been encouraging everyone to get remeasured."

She twisted the tape measure in her fingers and I felt my throat get tight. Black leather bracelet. Cute smirky smile.

I swallowed hard. "Half-cup?"

"Like, with shoes I'm a seven and a half. The same can be true with bras."

Seven and a half. Me too. What else could we have in common?

I nodded, trying to be casual. "Sure, why not?"

She took the bras from me, then held up the measuring tape again, that adorable smile on her face. She had a cute mole on her neck. There was an inch-long, light hair growing out of it.

I wanted to kiss it.

She had me take off my jacket, then stepped in close and wrapped her measuring tape around my ribcage, just under my boobs. My heart flipped. She leaned down to look closely at the number. I tried not to look down, but I could smell the strawberry shampoo in her hair. If I didn't have a shirt on, I could have felt her breath on my skin, and the thought made me curl my fingers into sweaty fists.

What I only realized later was that her fingers were inches from my two underwires. She might have been able to figure out the double-bra situation. That was definitely a more important thought to have had, but the fact that a cute girl was basically feeling me up made my brain foggy to any outside thoughts.

She jotted the number down on a pad on the podium, then hiked the tape right up on my boobs.

"Is this right over your nipples?" she asked, her shimmering eyes meeting mine.

"Yes." My voice was weak. She really had a knack for finding nipples.

"Take a deep breath, in and out." I managed to do that, somehow, and as I did, she loosened the tape just a bit. "Okay, great."

She adjusted the tape a little more. After working up the nerve for a few seconds, I asked, "Do you get a lot of 'buy me dinner first' jokes?"

She giggled. "People are getting better about not hitting on people in retail," she said to my tits. "Or, well.

Maybe it's just that not a lot of ladies want to buy me dinner."

Was that a sign? It felt like a sign. Or was it a sign not to? Or maybe the two underwires were cutting off the circulation to my brain.

"Really?"

"Really."

I laughed a little, my laugh sounding awkward and probably annoying. "That can't—that can't be true."

"It is." She cracked a smile. "In fact, unless I'm mistaken, you're the first."

It took a long time for that sentence to process in my mind through all the triple-firing synapses. I just stared in disbelief at the top of her head, my breath frozen. I was sure I misheard her, but couldn't for the life of me figure out what she must have *actually* said to me.

She looked up, and sudden terror crashed across her face, her eyes flinging open wide. "Oh god. Am I mistaken?"

I blinked. "What?"

She pulled the tape measure off me, began wrapping it tightly around her fingers. "Oh, no. I totally thought you were hitting on me. Shit. I'm so sorry if—"

"No, you—"

"—I was wrong, or made you uncomfortable—"

"No no no—"

"I really didn't mean to—"

"Wait—slow down."

This felt like driving in a snowstorm.

"You—" I smiled, laughed once, my whole face burning. "You were right. You were…right."

"I was? Oh god." She was smiling now, flirting again, tucking her soft chin into her chest. It made my body sparkle. "I'm so bad at this."

"You're not 'bad at this.' That, 'you're the first' line was smooth as fuck."

She smiled, her fingers fumbling with the tape measure again. Just then I noticed most of her fingers were wrapped up in flesh-colored bandages. Then suddenly her smile fell off her lips and she fell to a whisper. "Wait, how old are you?"

"Eighteen." I opted not to tell her how old I was yesterday.

She pressed a hand over her heart in relief. "I just turned twenty."

Twenty!! As if she wasn't intimidating enough.

"Is that okay?" I asked.

"If it's okay with you," she said back, and we·both giggled a bunch.

"So, um," I continued. "I work in the mall, too. Are you working tomorrow?"

"Twelve to seven. You?"

"Two to six. I can hang around after, though. Maybe we can meet at the food court?"

"Let's make it dinner."

Dinner. So grown up. "Sounds amazing."

"Meet me at the entrance of Pandora's Box and we'll go from there."

"Okay."

We hung in a still, heavenly glow, rosy and jittered. Then, "So you're a C and a half, by the way."

We both broke out into giggles again.

"Want me to get you some C and a halfs to try on?"

"Oh, no—no, thanks." If I could go back in time, I would have added, *I only came in to see the cute girl at the changing rooms, anyway.* That's what I came up with that night in bed, when I was replaying every moment of our conversation over and over and over again when I was supposed to be sleeping. Instead, all I really said was something like, "But thank you—now I know! C and a half. Nice. Cool."

We exchanged numbers before I left. I gave her my phone because I hadn't caught her name before. She typed her name and number into my contacts, and I did the same for her.

Elise. Elise. *Elise, Elise, Elise.*

I doodled her name on the back of a scrap bunny receipt until the end of my shift. Then I stole a new phone case to celebrate. It had ladybugs on it. Pretty cute.

Just like her.

Nine

On Being Yourself

So, I only told you that stuff because of what you said during our second session—that you can't tell my dad or the police that I smoke or drink. You said you can only talk about what I've told you if it seems like I'm going to hurt myself or someone else.

The shoplifting thing, I hope, doesn't count as something you have to report. The fact that I'm attracted to girls I hope also doesn't have to be reported, though I doubt it ever would. I was nervous to come out to you at first because I wasn't exactly "out" to the world yet, and especially not to my dad. When your dad owns a gun and leans right, politically, you tread carefully, even if he's progressive enough to understand mental health and stuff like that. I kept asking questions now and then about how he felt about queer stuff, but he was always pretty vague, which made me nervous to tell him.

When I got home, I turned to the side and stared at my two-bra'd silhouette in the mirror while I brushed my teeth. So that's what a C and a half would look like. Back in my room—cream walls covered in collages Claire and I created out of her mom's old magazines, a never-made twin bed with a checkered comforter, and a carpet of discarded clothes, makeup, and water bottles—I unhooked my new bra, folded it, and put it in my box of other stolen Pandora's Box trophies.

Someday, I thought, Elise and I would burn the lot of them, protesting the patriarchy *and* capitalism. I had to assume she agreed with that sentiment. She was too cool not to.

"Fuck that place," she'd say, throwing in her old work blazer. "I quit!"

"Yes! Fuckin' rebel!"

Then we'd make out on the ashes of the lingerie of the one percent and laugh that their attempt at a quick buck did nothing but soften the bed of two anarchist lesbians!

Or maybe she's a bisexual socialist. That's fine too. I'm open-minded.

The next day I was *way* too excited and nervous. I focused even less than usual during school, vacillating between daydreams about making out with her in the Pandora's Box changing room and minorly freaking out about all the ways I could completely mess up this date. And worrying about all the ways I've already embarrassed myself, and telling myself it must not have been all that bad if she agreed to go out with me anyway. At work, Max put me on camera, because the Easter season was ramping up and he was training a new hire on the cash register. Her name was Kathi and she was alright, just pretty bubbly. She was also older than me, somewhere in her twenties, so Max was training her to open and close. Apparently, since Max was the only person able to do either at the moment, he needed to find someone who could, or he wouldn't have a single day off the whole season.

At around 4:30, Max asked me to escort Billy back for his break.

I figured things would be weird between me and Billy, since this was the first time we would be alone together again since he caught me stealing, but they weren't.

"Want a cigarette, Ladybug?" he asked as soon as we got to Max's office and he took off the bunny head. Sweat lined his forehead. "Looks like you need one."

"Ladybug?" He gestured toward my new phone case, which was, of course, covered in red and orange ladybugs. "Oh! Gotcha. No, thank you."

It felt suddenly disrespectful to enjoy myself around him, but mostly I didn't want to smell too much like smoke, in case Elise didn't like it. We sat in our usual seats, me on the stool, him in Max's chair. I found my Dr. Pepper and fruit leather in my bag and got to enjoying my break—I was dying to get back to Blocki. I top the local leaderboards, like, daily. Sometimes I see multicolored cubes exploding on my ceiling when I'm trying to get to sleep.

"I just mean you look like you've got something on your mind."

"Oh, no," I said in a soft, high-pitched voice reserved for authority. I opened Blocki. "Just tired."

"Mhm. Plans later?"

"Just homework."

"Bullshit."

I looked up from my game. Billy had his bunny feet up, crossed on Max's desk.

"What? I have homework."

"Yeah, maybe, but that's not all. Come on, I can tell."

I figured he was only doing this to get me back on his side. I hated how some adults flipped between being cool and acting like parents whenever they felt like it. It's like they had no idea how to act around teenagers. But I did like Billy, and I did want the validation of having a guy with face tattoos as a work friend. Claire and John and…well, *those* two, anyway, would find it pretty badass.

So, I said, "Well, actually, I have a date."

"Oh, fun! With who?"

I weighed all the variables—his age, his local accent, his tattoos, the fact that I was closer to the exit and had my phone in my hand—and deemed it safe to say, "This cute girl named Elise who works at Pandora's Box. I met her yesterday before my shift."

Billy didn't skip a beat. "Nice! Where you going?"

I exhaled in relief. "I don't know yet. Dinner someplace."

"So, you're nervous?"

"A little." Beyond belief.

Billy took down his legs. "Have you gone on dates before?"

"I dated this boy, Chris, freshman year, but for reasons now obvious, we didn't work out."

"So this is your first date with a girl!" I smiled into my chest, feeling Billy's eyes trying to catch mine. "Damn. No wonder you're so excited. When I had my first date with a girl I nearly threw up. Never mind how nerve-wracking it must be for an LGBTQ+ individual. Lots of pressure, I'm sure."

I almost blurted out laughing at "LGBTQ+ individual." Not that it was wrong, just that he sounded like an eighties after-school special. Kind of like you and your "online computer games." He was trying, though, and that's more than most people.

"You're right," I said, disguising the laugh I couldn't completely muffle as one of nervous resignation. "It's just, I've dreamed of dating a girl for so long, and now it's finally happening. I'm nervous."

"Is she cute?"

"She is *insanely* cute. Oh my god. These dreadlocks and cute glasses, and this little mole right here."

"Shit. You must be hella nervous."

"I *am!*" I shut off my phone and slipped it in my back pocket. Billy leaned on his bunny elbows. His skull shading distorted when he raised his eyebrows into a smile. "She's a little older," I went on. "Which just adds to it. Ugh, I'm totally going to mess this up."

"I'm sure you're not."

"And I just so very much want it to work out. There're basically no other queer people around here."

"Really?"

"Well, I'm sure they exist, but they don't exist at my school. Or they're hiding, like me. Or they're gay for a week and kiss you and make you like them and then change their mind."

He blinked in exaggerated surprise. "Wow. I take it there's a story to that one?"

"Uh, yeah. Straight girls suck."

"I hear you. Except my girlfriend, she's cool. And a few other people, I'm sure, are straight and cool." He twisted his mouth, teasing me just a little bit.

"I mean, a *bunch* of people, I guess," I agreed, faking a disgruntled pout. "But a lot of them suck for being so, so pretty and so, so *straight*."

Billy smirked at the table, tapped some ash in the trash can. "But this girl isn't straight."

"Definitely not. Thank god."

"And she *is* pretty."

"And smart, and interesting, and funny, and a bunch of other stuff, too. But yes, she's so pretty."

My god, so pretty.

"Well, hey, I'm rooting for you. And just be yourself. I know you've heard that before, but—can I tell you a story?" Then, before I could say anything, he continued: "I didn't tell my girlfriend I liked *The Golden Girls* until we were already dating for a year. You know *The Golden Girls?*"

"That sitcom with the old ladies?"

"Yeah!" Then he sang, "*Thank you for being a friend!* I love that shit. It's the funniest show. My grandmother and I would die laughing, watching it together. Anyway. One day my girlfriend walked in on me watching Blanche and Dorothy upstage each other at the Rusty Anchor—you remember that one?"

I shook my head, and his jaw dropped dramatically.

"It's like the best one. You're missing out. Really. We

should have a marathon. I'll see if I can get some on my phone for next break. You'd like them, I know you would. I—gosh. I could go on for hours, but, anyway. She walked in on me watching *Golden Girls,* and you know what happened?"

"She dumped you?"

He smiled sagely. "She told me that she used to watch the show all the time with her nana. And she loved it. And I told her I used to watch it all the time with *my* grandmother, and *I* love it! And now we watch it all the time together, curled up with some chips and her little dog. We sing the theme song together and stuff. And we'd never have done that if she never walked in on me. I would have watched it in shameful secret the rest of my life, and we never would have had those moments together. Anyway, the good people out there will never dump you for watching *The Golden Girls,* even if they didn't used to watch it with their nana. Like—what's something weird that you do?"

Besides shoplift? I stalled, folding the wrapper over the remaining half of the fruit leather and tucking it back in my bag. "I watch old movies."

"Come on, that's not that weird."

"I work with the Easter Bunny."

He laughed at that, but kept pressing.

"Um, fine. I make dolls."

"You play with dolls?"

"I *make* dolls." God, I'm not *that* weird. "Of cartoon characters. Scooby Doo and Spongebob, The Powerpuff Girls. I make them, sew them. Hang on—" I pulled out my phone again and scrolled back to find a photo. I finally found one from a few months ago of a set of dolls I made for Nora, of Pac-Man and the four ghosts. Billy pinched the screen to zoom in and out, oohing and ahhing.

"You made this? How?"

"Just kinda cut out the fabric and…yeah. Sewed 'em."

"No pattern?"

"No. But these were easy. You should have seen the Bart Simpson one I did a couple years ago. I can try to find a picture." I took the phone back and scrolled awhile, then handed it back.

"Holy crap, Ladybug, this is amazing."

It was a pretty good one. I had managed to get some pretty stiff, felt-like yellow fabric and then sewed that over a few sheets of cardboard to get his hair to stand up stiffly. I'd used a light off-white on the eyes so they looked alive, and the arms were poseable—the first time I'd figured out how to do that without weighing them down too much. The mouth and pupils were embroidered, and the shoes even slid on and off. I was pretty proud of this one. He was in my closet, the centerpiece of my multi-copyrighted collection.

"She'll love this."

I snatched the phone back, shoved it back in my pocket. "Ha. No, no way. It's way too dorky, she'd like, run away from me if I showed her this."

"Oh, come on. You told *me!*"

"Well, I'm not trying to impress you." Anymore.

"My girlfriend liked *The Golden Girls*. Be yourself!"

Yeah, sure, "be yourself," but that's too simplistic, to be honest. More accurate would be "be a version of yourself who is cool enough for Elise and who doesn't spend a stupid amount of time making dolls of cartoon characters." But I smiled, because how could I argue against "be yourself?"

"And have confidence," he added, and that sat a little better with me.

Regardless, there was no way in hell I was going to tell Elise I made dolls. I was going to stick to my normal hobbies—how I like Kubrick and Hitchcock movies, how I ride my bike (though I hardly have since getting my car), and how I hang out with my friends. My "weird" will be how I work for the Easter Bunny. That's weird enough. That's enough of "being myself" for one date.

I won't drag you through the whole date. Nothing's more boring than hearing someone talk about a first date, but I'll give you the highlights. I went through all five stages of grief over being stood up in the two minutes she was late, sure that she somehow knew I was stealing and this was all a big prank, or that she changed her mind at the last minute, or that she found something embarrassing I posted online four years ago or something and bailed—but it all brushed aside the moment she ran out of the store and pulled me right into a hug. She still smelled like strawberries. I wrapped my arms around her quick, let go half a second later. I could still feel the ghost of her body against my own.

"Oh, my gosh. *So* sorry I'm late, my boss just went on like, a tirade because someone apparently shoplifted one of the seasonal items and—" she waved her hand past her forehead. "I just can't keep up. Hooligans. Anyway. I have no idea if you have to deal with that bullshit. I suppose it'd be hard to steal photos."

I laughed a bit too loudly, praying I looked natural. *Shit*, my hands were sweating. *They noticed? It was a special bra?! Does she know?* My tummy flipped and twisted in on itself.

If I were in a movie, I would have said, "People steal the frames, sometimes," cool and mysterious. Foreshadowing. But I'm not in a movie, so I just stuttered out, "Yeah, no, not really. Thankfully, yeah."

We walked down to The Cheesecake Factory, fluttering through conversation about crazy customers we encountered that day at work and both of our crazy bosses. She got a hoot out of my impression of Max, and I tried to put aside the shoplifting thing for now and focus on her.

Turns out, focusing on Elise wasn't very hard to do.

When we got the menus, I found out she's a vegetarian, which is something I'd always wanted to be. I considered saying I was one, too, and then just sticking with it, but I took Billy's advice and was "myself."

"I've thought about doing the same," I said.

Then she talked about vegetarian recipes, and I found out she likes to cook, which is cool because I like to bake sometimes. She said next time we should eat in and cook and bake for each other. That's right. "Next time." I could hardly breathe through that smile.

She likes old movies, too, and we talked about *Rear Window* for a crazy long time. When I mentioned Kubrick, she said she'd somehow never seen *The Shining*, and I suggested we do that after we eat in. I couldn't exactly picture her jumping in fright into my arms, but I *could* picture her loving the cinematography. She seemed like the kind of person who would catch a bunch of background details that went right over my head.

Basically, there was lots of sweating and giggling on my part, lots of being interesting and cool and funny and pretty on Elise's part. Sometimes I told jokes that she pretended to laugh at, and that made me want to stab myself with the butterknife, but other times I could tell her laughs were genuine, and over time, as I realized that it was actually kind of going well, the genuine laughs came out more and more. I ate half my salad without realizing it—probably the most I'd eaten for one meal in months. And I told her the softball story, too—the one I told you on our first meeting, when I ran around the bases the wrong way. I also didn't tell her the Mom part of the story. Which is why she laughed.

And I didn't tell her about the dolls, obviously. I'm not an idiot. But she did get a kick out of my job, and she said her niece would love to get a photo with an Easter Bunny, and that maybe she'd bring her in on one of her days off. I said that would be great, and felt a little silly about getting excited over seeing Elise for an extra two minutes in the middle of a shift. *Was that too excited? Too much, too soon?*

Like I said, in hindsight, it went well—but somehow, I left The Cheesecake Factory half convinced I blew it. We walked out to the parking lot together. She had parked on the left, closer to Pandora's Box, and I had parked on the right. There on the sidewalk we kind of faltered, hesitating, two feet apart but not touching. She turned to face me directly, but I found I couldn't meet her eyes.

"I'd love to see you again, Mo," Elise said, her voice dipping into a whisper on my name. I was floored. I just smiled dumbly, still looking somewhere by my shoes, trying to think of the right thing to say. Then she lifted my chin with her forefinger and added, "And I'd like to kiss you now. If that's okay."

Hooooly shit.

I blinked a bunch, swallowing and smiling for a millisecond before I said, "Me too." My mouth pulled together into a nervous pout. I closed my eyes and leaned in, just a bit.

Then she kissed me, and my hands flew to her waist. She was so soft, and tasted like strawberries, and almost made me melt into a puddle on the floor. She pulled away too soon and my mind stopped working.

"Wow," I whispered.

She laughed, and we hugged and laughed together, and then kissed one more time, and then she squeezed my hand and headed off to her car.

Gahhh! It was so awesome. I squealed the whole car ride home, forced to believe the impossible, like an atheist dying and waking up in heaven. *That…actually went well. Oh my god, that actually went well. I kissed her, and it actually went well!*

Then my smile dropped off my face. Oh, god. I kissed a girl, right in front of the mall. Dad was off work, but what was I thinking? He could have been called in, or one of his buddies would have seen, or…

"Shit." I gripped the steering wheel tighter. *So, okay, no more dates at the mall. I'll just pretend everything's fine, and…*

it will either all be fine, or blow up in my face. Either way, I thought, because all the worries in the world couldn't keep my giddiness down, *we kissed. This might actually work out. If I don't fuck it up.*

By the time I parked at home, I already had a text from her. *Thanks for a great dinner! Hope to do it again sometime....:)*

Me too! I typed back.

I was still fumbling with my keys when she replied: *Yay! Next time I promise to be on time (unless another dummy steals a bra :P)*

Ugh. That made all my tummy nervousness come back. And I was in such a good mood. Of course, even when I hadn't fucked something up, I'd fucked it up. I stuffed my phone away and ran inside. Dad waved and said he'd made dinner. He was at the kitchen table, eating spaghetti and jarred alfredo sauce in a deep bowl Mom used to insist was only for soup, for some reason.

"Already ate, thanks."

I tried to slip by, but he stopped me. "Hey, how goes the job so far?"

"Um, great."

"You're liking it?"

"Yup."

"Good...and, that lady you're talking to...?"

That's what he called you. "That lady I'm talking to." I think he did it for my sake, as if I was afraid of the word "therapist."

"Yeah, I like her." I smiled, nodded, glanced at the stairs. "So, um. I've got some homework, so."

"Yeah!" he swallowed quick, wiped at his mouth with a paper napkin. "Yep! Go ahead. I won't keep you." He smiled, mouth still half full, worried crinkles at the edges of his eyes. "Study hard!"

"You bet." I tried to give a genuine smile, but it probably looked as uncomfortable as his.

Anyway. I got upstairs and pulled out that bra I stole the day before, and saw that, yup, the sewn-on tag (not a security tag—it didn't have one of those) mentioned that it was a Spring Collection special. It was just laying on a table! I hadn't noticed it was expensive, or special. Usually, the nice stuff was lacy and complicated and hanging up. I felt nervous tingles along the back of my neck.

Well. Whatever. She won't find out. I just won't steal from Pandora's Box again, then. It's all good.

Yeah. I was a *genius*.

Ten

Just a Debate

The next day I was super hyped to thank Billy for his advice. After the first rush there was no one for a while so I went over to his eggshell throne and smiled into his dead bunny eyes.

"Dude, thank you so much for your advice yesterday. I was nervous, but it went really well!" He didn't reply, so I kept going. "Thanks for giving me a good pep talk for it."

"Oh, that's great."

Well, he seemed less than enthused. I told him some details—how she thought it was funny that I worked here and how we liked the same old movies.

"And, not to brag, but we *did* kiss a little which was—" I made the OK sign and clicked my tongue. "—*pretty* great."

"Sounds awesome. You'll have to tell me all about it. Hey, can we talk about this at break?"

"Oh. Um, yeah, sure."

I gave another smile and looked behind the creamy blue, mesh bunny eyes to see Billy's. They were staring past and above me, up to the second floor.

I turned back around and headed toward cash. Kathi and Max were set to come in in about an hour (we were getting afternoon "rushes" now and needed all hands on deck), so for the moment it was just me and Billy. I followed his gaze to the second floor, trying to make it look nonchalant.

It was my dad, talking to three tattooed men in hoodies who rested their elbows on the chrome railing. My dad laughed, but I could see, even from this far away, the tenseness in his eyes, the tightness in his jaw. He held his hands on his belt, kind of normal, kind of implying he had a gun. Doing the ol' "mall cop check-in with the sketchy people" technique, I guess. I knew he was acting, for sure. Dad hates gangs, and hates everyone who looks like they might be in a gang—because of the whole "Mom" thing— so he'd never just be hanging out with these people.

Actually, to be honest, he probably would have flipped out if he knew what Billy looked like while I was working with him.

The hoodie guys laughed with Dad, then one of them looked away from my dad and over the rail and right down at the bunny set with a fading smile. He was sucking on what looked like a cigarette, but when he moved his hand away, he pulled a round, purple lollipop away from his mouth.

His hand out of the way, I saw, tattooed on his chin, a big bird with wings flying up his cheeks.

A weird uneasiness crept across my shoulders. I didn't know why, really, and maybe I was just as prejudiced as my dad, who was obviously only making his presence known to these guys because they had a bunch of tattoos, and my dad associated tattoos with gangs. If I knew anything from talking with Billy, it was that guys with tattoos didn't necessarily mean trouble. But these guys...the way the guy with the lollipop stared, hard and dark at the set before smacking on a casual smile to turn back to my dad...it was giving me the creeps. Obviously, they were giving Billy the creeps, too, which was even creepier. If they even scared Billy...

I knew not to make it obvious. I also knew I'd have to ask Kathi ASAP if I could escort Billy to his break, because I needed answers on that, bad. By the time she actually got to work, the gangsters (because they had to be gangsters, right?) were long gone.

Kathi was always about as agreeable as she found necessary. She hated the camera (the back end of it, anyway—you should see her Instagram) so once I agreed to take over for the rest of the shift, she graciously surrendered the first break.

Two hours later, I finally closed the break room door behind Billy, who quickly whipped off the bunny head. I could smell the sweat, like onions. I stalled a little while he got comfy. I didn't really know how to bring it up.

"So," I started, fishing around my bag for today's snack—a Ziplock of Cheez-its. "Elephant in the room. Who were those guys?"

"What guys?"

He said it so naturally I questioned whether or not I had imagined it.

"The guys on the second floor, talking to my dad."

"Your dad?"

"The mall cop?"

Billy nodded, but his face was still indecipherable. "I didn't know he was your dad."

"Well, he is."

"Oh." He frowned a little, scratched the side of his face. Also stalling. "They're just some guys. I—"

"You said you weren't in a gang."

He paused, meeting my gaze. "I'm *not*," he spat out, hitting the "T" hard. A flash of the Billy who confronted me about the picture frame flared in his eyes. "Look, can we just not talk about it?"

"Um—"

"Let's talk about your date instead. It went well; you said you took my advice?"

I think we both knew that discussion wasn't over, but what could I do? To be honest, I was a little afraid to push him. So, while he uncharacteristically fumbled to get his lighter going, I perched on my usual stool and dug around for a Cheez-it, trying to act like such a change in subject was normal and like I didn't feel totally berated.

"I did. Confidence, being myself."

"Did you tell her about the dolls?"

"No."

"I'm telling you, you gotta!"

A fake smile kept floating up to the surface of Billy's face, but it didn't reach his skull-shaded eyes. I couldn't stop comparing his tattoos to the one on the other guy's chin. They had the same strong boldness, same vibe. I know I only saw the other guy's from like fifty feet away, but even so, I would have bet they were done by the same artist.

"That Bart Simpson one you showed me?" Billy went

on, moving his hands more than usual. "Shit. I'd pay money for that. It's skills, man."

"Maybe." I shifted, munched some Cheez-its, offered him some. He took a handful. Too many to be polite, really, but he was nervous and I was never going to eat that many Cheez-its all at once, anyway.

I couldn't let the topic go. "So, you're really not gonna tell me about those guys? I mean, it's cool if you don't want to, but—"

He sighed. "It's not even that I don't want to, it's…" he ran a hand over his chin, "…I can't. It's not like your dolls, it's like your depression."

"…my what?"

"Or whatever you go to therapy for. Some stuff you just can't talk about."

So, here's the thing. It's not like I *wasn't* scared of Billy, a little. I mean, we were in a room alone, he was obviously sketchy, and he was twice my size, so I didn't want to piss him off. But sometimes my emotions seem to take over my head and my mouth, and this was one of those times.

Before I knew it, I said to him, "'Can't?' Some stuff you don't *want* to talk about, more like."

He laughed once, but I could tell he didn't mean it. He bit at his lower lip. "Just drop it."

"But—"

"It's over, it's done with, and I'm not going to talk about it."

"It's not over if they're here, staring at you at work."

"Mo? Drop it," he repeated, and looked like he meant it. I looked away, too annoyed to even nod. "Sometimes people don't want to talk about their past. Sometimes they just want to not think about it and try to be a better person and move on."

I put the Cheez-its back. I wasn't hungry anymore. Jesus, he was really starting to sound like Nora. She was like that all the time before our fight in the treehouse, always kind of moping around, looking sad, and then acting like the depth of her problems was incomprehensible to us mere mortals. I like helping people—but how do you help people who don't want to be helped?

How do *you* do it? I'm sure you get people who don't want to be helped all the time. How do you get them to open up to you and talk to you? And how were we supposed to actually feel bad for her or give her advice or do *anything* if she never told us what was actually wrong?

After my shift, around six p.m., I went over to Claire's to hang out with her and John. She didn't have a birthday present for me, and I pretended that that didn't worry me.

After we smoked in her treehouse, we all kind of wandered around the woods for a while, trying to enjoy one of the first truly decent Saturday evenings of the year. The woods behind Claire's house is pretty big; she lives right against these trails that ring the golf course. Sometimes we can find golf balls back there, when we end up closer to the course, but not too often.

The woods are really nice, full of pine and oak trees and soft green ferns, just starting to grow again. Right then, the sun was about an hour away from setting and our boots were all pretty loud, smacking wetly against the dirt and leaves. While we walked, I bitched about Nora, and they both kind of hummed now and then but didn't say anything. The weed was kicking in, and the cool breeze felt nice on my face—not quite cold, not quite spring—and I shut up for a minute to enjoy the feeling of air shooting in and out of my lungs.

John started talking about his cousins in Seattle again. Apparently, they went with their parents to the legal weed stores they have all over the place out there, and their parents bought the family a thing of edibles. I scrunched up my face a little. I still found it a little weird that there were kids out there who got high with their parents. I wondered, then, if my mom might have done the same with me. Eventually, if she were still alive as I got older, she probably would have. I had no idea if she smoked weed ever, but I had to imagine she did. It would be kind of weird if she didn't.

Then again, Dad would never. He was way too...Dad. So maybe not.

By then we'd reached the back creek and the little wood-pallet bridge Claire and her old friend, Dina, had made in middle school. It was safer now to just leap over, despite the gripping mud, because the pallet was so weather-beaten and bug-eaten the weight of a high schooler would render it to splinters. But it stayed there anyway, and it was kind of nostalgic, even though I hadn't made it. It reminded me of stuff I did in middle school, back in the city. And of the meadow story, but I think I've told you that already.

Claire and Dina had picked a good spot for a bridge. The rocks nearby were good for sitting on, and the pebbles good for throwing, and the long-dead branches of the big oak were good for starting small, illegal fires (which John set to doing) and poking out dead leaves from between rocks to make the creek flow more strongly (which I chose to do). Claire sat on a rock and started slowly rolling another joint, and it was pretty peaceful for a while. The sun filtered through the branches and striped us all like zebras.

"You know," Claire said, thought better of it, then repeated with firmness, "You know, *we* still like Nora."

I shoved a clump of brown oak leaves downriver. I felt bitter at even the mention of her name. "I know."

"I just mean, I don't think it's really fair to shit on her just because you're fighting with her right now."

"I'm—yeah. I'm just—"

"I think it's fine to…vent," added John, who was kneeling on a patch of underbrush over a thinly smoking pile of tinder. "And that's fine, if you want to vent."

John's such an idiot. He didn't even know half of the story, but of course he *had* to throw his two cents in.

"It's just, she's our friend. And yours, too, you know?"

"Well, I don't know if *that's* still true," I said, trying to make it sound like I didn't care one way or the other, like if we were talking about football. "She was really mad at me."

A little worm was on one of the leaves. He squiggled around and tried to crawl quickly back underwater.

"I mean. Yeah. It's not like you didn't give her reason to be mad, though."

I stabbed at the leaf and made it sink. The worm sunk to the bottom. "I dunno about that."

"I mean. Mo," Claire said in a "don't be stupid" voice

that made me look up from the worm in the creek. "You basically said her shitty parents weren't anything to complain about."

I took a step onto a river rock nearly the size of my shoe so I could reach another clump of leaves. "I still stand by that," I said, quieter.

"And that's fine," said John.

"Well, it's clearly not 'fine,' if we're talking about it. If you're like, staging an intervention about it."

"I mean, okay, you're right," Claire said, kind of cutting me off. "She never tells us what's going on, so it's annoying when she acts like she wants to talk about it, and then—"

"She wants *attention*," I said, "rather than she wants to 'talk' about it. Because if she talked about it, it would be obvious that she actually has nothing to complain about."

Claire sighed. It felt good to be bitchy right then, to openly complain about Nora, but I knew I had to stop. If Claire dumped me as a friend, so would John, and then I'd be down to no friends at all. Except the Easter Bunny at the mall, I guess. And that's just sad.

I took a deep breath, trying to calm my rising anger.

"Maybe she's exaggerating," Claire said. I rolled my eyes at the creek. "Everybody exaggerates sometimes. But on the other hand, maybe she just can't tell us the truth yet, for some reason."

"Well, she should."

"Why?"

"Because we're her friends."

"It's not like everyone has to tell their friends

everything," John piped up again. "Do *you* tell *us* everything?"

I mean, John didn't know *anything*, but I didn't even tell Claire some of my stuff. Like about going to therapy, obviously.

"No."

"Then, I dunno. Maybe she was right to be upset."

"Well, so am I!" I shoved my poking stick deep in the mud, worked it under a stuck rock. "Whatever her parents do, they're together—" I pointed at Claire, who stared back like a statue. "And alive." I pointed at myself. "And super accepting, so Nora has no right to complain, because it's not nearly as bad as Claire and I have it."

"Okay, first of all, sometimes it's better for parents to split up than it is for them to stay together," Claire said. "Like, it sucked, but in the end, I'm glad my parents split up. They hated each other. But either way, it's not a competition—"

"Exactly! It's not even a competition; we obviously have it worse!" And I had it worse than Claire, but I knew not to bring that up at the moment or risk ruining my whole argument.

"That's not what I meant! God, are you even listening? I *mean*, it's not a competition. You can't compare peoples' situations and say one *isn't* bad just because another is quote-unquote worse."

Oh my God. "Yes, you can. You obviously can. That's like saying you can't tell the difference between a papercut and getting your arm chopped off."

"Then maybe none of us should ever complain, because

we're not starving orphans in the middle of a war, like, dying of leprosy. Or slaves or some shit." Claire wasn't rolling the joint anymore, and I wasn't poking in the river. We were kind of glaring at each other from ten feet away. "Someone always has it worse. So what? Is no one ever allowed to complain except the one person on earth who has it the worst? Just because someone's gotten their arm cut off means I can never complain about a papercut?"

"Oh, come on, you know that's not what I meant."

"It *is*, though. You feel like no one who 'has it better' than *you*, specifically, has a right to complain about their lives."

"*No*, I just feel like Nora shouldn't complain about her mom, because at least she has a mom. That's it."

"Okay, whatever."

"Yeah, *whatever*. You know I'm right."

Claire licked the joint closed and stood up to light it on John's tiny fire.

"Let's change the subject," John said quietly, tossing on another twig.

And we did, to nothing important at all. Claire discussed how nervous she was over an orchestra concert, and John talked about how his parents might sell their summer home—the privileged fuck. Nothing real, nothing deep, nothing serious. And really, it wasn't super awkward—after we got through the joint, anyway. But still, I felt a weirdness when I went to leave and neither of them reached to hug me, or even fist-bump me.

I told myself it wasn't that awkward. That they weren't

mad at me, that it was just a discussion. A debate. That I was overthinking. That I was just high.

...I almost believed myself.

Eleven

The next day was Sunday, and I had my first early-morning shift of the Easter season. I couldn't stop replaying the conversation I had with Claire and John in my head, trying to come up with better comebacks and stronger arguments. I aimed the sleepy camera at kids still picking at their church clothes, half terrified of the bunny, half bored of it.

"I know he's just a helper," a little boy proudly declared to me on his way out. "He's not the real bunny."

Max saved the day on that one, rushing in from the cash register station. "Shh. We don't wanna ruin it for the little kids, right? Can you keep this big-kid secret?"

The kid sparkled, then theatrically locked his lips with a key. Max got a tip in the egg-shaped tip jar for that one.

"Quick thinking," I said. He turned around, open-mouthed, then nodded, as if he just remembered what I was talking about.

"Oh. Yeah." He smiled and waved a hand dismissively. "You develop a bag of tricks after working with kids awhile. Animals, too."

"You mean the bunny?"

He smirked. "On the off-season, I raise and sell alpacas."

"Alpacas?"

"You know, like llamas, but not assholes."

What the actual *hell?* I had a thousand questions, but then a slew of customers came, and I was busy until Billy's morning break.

"Did you hear Max say he raises and sells alpacas?"

Billy snorted, easing into peak break posture. Today he had a panini, and he took the first satisfyingly crunchy bite. "Yeah. He told me his life story and then some during my interview. Didn't he tell you?"

"My interview was more of a formality."

"He not only breeds and sells alpacas, but he flips houses, *and* he runs an exotic, ex-circus animal rehabilitation center in Wyoming."

"Huh. I wouldn't have expected any of that."

"*And* he has six foster kids. Dude's a machine."

"Jeez! Nobody tells me anything!"

I said it as a joke, but as it hung in the air, a bitter taste spread in my mouth, no matter how many banana chips I ate. I was thinking of Nora. And I was thinking about Claire and John, who had their little couple code where they can communicate without words, and that's fine, but Claire and I used to have that, and now she doesn't tell me anything, either. The way John said, "you don't tell *us* everything," as if me telling Claire meant automatically telling him, too. Which, well, at this point it did. And it's not like I didn't go to Claire, and Nora, and even John when Mom died. I mean, she was already dead when I met them, but even so, I talked to them about it for days, weeks. And they helped me. And they were cool about it.

But over time, I stopped talking about my problems, too—partly because they stopped telling me theirs, and partly because I was so intensely grateful to be out of that all-encompassing grief, I felt I could handle anything on my own. I was resilient. I knew a real problem from an exaggerated one.

Mom dying? Real problem.

Stressed out by deciding on a college? Dad's angry at you? Your review of *Psycho* wasn't admitted into the school newspaper? Lost your tickets to a one-night, big-screen showing of *2001: A Space Odyssey* you've been looking forward to for weeks? Exaggerated. Fake. Get over it, I'd tell myself. No use telling anybody, it would just waste their time while they judged you for being all worked up over nothing. I'll get through it.

I've been through far worse.

"Lost in space, Ladybug?"

I gazed at Billy in confusion. "Yeah, um." I shook my head, smiled, turned on my phone and opened Blocki. "It's nothing."

"Can't be 'nothing.'"

"Well, it's nothing—" important. Earth-shattering. Worth talking about. "—big."

"Small soup still cooks in a big pot."

"…what?"

"My grandmother used to say that. Just because it's small doesn't mean I don't want to hear it."

Blocki finally loaded up, and I had my thumb hovered over the New Game button. So, he won't tell me anything big—about his tattoos, about the gangsters on the second floor—but he wanted me to tell him something little. I closed my phone.

"Why are you so bent on helping me?"

He tilted his head a little. "What do you mean?"

"I mean, I clearly pissed you off yesterday, so—but, even if I didn't. Do you want to be a therapist or something?"

He furrowed his brow and sunk his teeth into the crunchy panini. I waited while he chewed and eventually swallowed.

"I like helping you."

"Why?"

"Because…I was a major dick when I was younger, and I have some karma I need to balance out." He waited. I waited. Then he looked away and continued. "I used to hang out with a rough crowd. And whenever any of them talked about their past, I realized something—they all needed someone to talk to. It sounds kind of dumb, but it's true. I realized it myself, when I finally got my own ass in therapy. No matter what the problem is, it's worse when you don't talk about it."

I raised one eyebrow.

"For real. So I try to talk to everybody I encounter on a typical basis. Makes the silent bunny job hard, but—you, my girlfriend, Max, that new girl Kathi, the nice lady at the laundromat. If I just talk to you and I'm a friend, maybe I can make it so you, or him, or her, or whoever feel like they…you know, have a friend. And I kind of feel like every time I talk to someone about whatever's bugging them, I get a little more good karma. Like—" he made a sprinkling motion with his fingers, "—*Pring-pring,* more good karma points. And maybe someday I'll feel like it's cancelled out all the bad shit I did."

I couldn't raise my one eyebrow any higher, so I tilted my chin to get the same effect.

"What?"

"So, you think talking out your problems is the best medicine? Talking to your friends can solve all your problems?"

"Yeah."

"This coming from the guy who totally dodged my question about the sketchy gangsters yesterday?"

He narrowed his eyes and took another big bite, but shook his head playfully as he chewed. "Nice try. I'm the doctor here, Ladybug, I'm the one who needs the good karma. You first. Tell me what's on your mind."

Oh, I had a hundred sassy responses locked and loaded, but I set them aside. It was a nice conversation, but he was right—something was bugging me. And he was beginning to make talking out my problems sound like a win/win. Even if it was something small. A papercut, not an amputation.

"Basically—and I know this is dumb, because it's just Max, but it's not just Max—thing is, why didn't I know about the alpacas?" I pulled up my leg by the heel of my boot onto the stool, under my other thigh. "God, it's stupid. I just feel like nobody tells me anything."

Billy twisted his lips up. "I had to pull teeth for you to tell me you have a date."

"I—there's a difference between the important things and things that just waste time to talk about."

"I don't know about that. Things only feel important when they happen to you," Billy said. "Like…prom. Your prom couldn't matter less to me, but it will be super important to you." I rolled my eyes, and he added quickly, "Or, maybe not prom, but something else you care about. Your date, for instance, is only *really* big to you. But I still like hearing about it."

"I guess."

Billy chuckled again. "I don't mean to insult you. Even if you know it's worth it, it's hard to open up to people. You know that from therapy. It takes a while. My girlfriend has incredible patience. She charmed my stories out of me like a snake."

"But you're a bunny," I deadpanned. He slapped his knee, eyes wide in equally sarcastic laughter, which soon broke to real giggles.

"Why don't we practice with each other? We don't have to get into the big stuff right away, or at all—like I said, the small stuff is just as important. We can just talk to each other about our lives. Get used to opening up to people, and then other people will open up to us, too. One story each a day."

"To practice talking about ourselves?"

"Yeah. Why not?"

"You just want the good karma," I said. "A bit selfish. Doesn't doing something good only for the good karma kind of cancel it out?"

That one seemed to take him by surprise. He stopped

chewing for a sec, then swallowed hard. "No. I don't know, doesn't matter. It'll be good for both of us, like bonus therapy, but without the crying. And the copays."

Yeah. I thought I caught him say that earlier, and now it was confirmed. He's in therapy, too.

I sucked on my teeth a little, considering. There was a lot about Billy I wanted to know—like who the gangsters were who were talking to my dad, and why Billy thinks I'm stupid enough to believe a dude with those tattoos wasn't in a crazy dangerous gang, and how he was allowed to leave (that is, if he told the truth about not currently being in a gang).

"We'll probably never see each other again after Easter, anyway," he added. "Because shit—I am *not* sweating my ass off in this suit and scaring babies for two months again next year."

"Hm. I'm in," I said, sitting up in my chair. "Might help me on me and Elise's second date."

"You got a second date!"

"Tonight."

He put down his panini, making crumbs scatter across Max's desk, and gave me a bona-fide fist bump. I caught a better look at the tattoo on the back of his hand this time— a cross, but instead of Jesus it looked to be a fly, or maybe a bee that was being crucified.

"Hell yeah! Good for you!"

"Thanks."

"But that doesn't count as a story."

I thought long and hard, but my memory seemed as blank and boring as an IKEA side table.

Finally, I settled on the time we—Claire, John, Nora, and I—tried to find the meadow. I think I might have told you this story, but I can't remember. I tell it a lot. You can just skip the next bit if you've heard it before.

"Maybe half a mile down the street from my friend John's house, there was this meadow," I began. "He didn't know it was there. We discovered it on Google Earth one day, when Claire and I were using it to look up our friends' addresses. Behind this big white house—John lives in a huge house, too—was a big, grassy meadow. Well, it looked like a meadow.

"We started planning a picnic. It was so *novel*, the idea of being anywhere alone without parents around. We could go on walks—this was before we could drive, we were maybe thirteen or fourteen—but we all lived in the suburbia sprawl. Nothing was within walking distance. And I really missed that, coming from Somerville. Mostly we hung out in the woods behind Claire's. We still mostly do that, but it was buggy, wet, and cold, and her parents didn't like us to go deeper than where they could see from the house.

"But a meadow and a picnic. No parents. It was a dream, at thirteen.

"We got some stuff together. I remember Claire was adamant that we needed rope, in case it was a bog and we started to sink in it. John brought his Boy Scout knife. Nora and I brought the food. We hiked through untouched forest between these two huge suburban McMansions to arc over into the meadow. John was in the lead, swatting at ivy with his dinky knife.

"Then John stopped. We all stopped behind him.

'Cattails,' he said, just like that. 'Cattails.' Yeah, so? Cattails?

"'It's a fucking swamp,' he said.

"We had a whole picnic packed up in Nora's backpack, a knife, and fifty feet of rope, but our meadow was a swamp."

I smiled, laughed a little at the memory.

"So, what did you learn?"

I laughed again. "Um, I learned that swamps look like meadows on Google Earth."

"No!" Billy said, still playful, but less so. "What did it teach you? That's part of the story. How did you change?"

That took almost as much work as thinking up a good story. I tried to shrug him off with a, "What is this, English class?" but he held firm.

I sighed out a big puff of air, making some curly wisps of my side bangs dance.

"I guess it taught me not to assume the best. Just because something looks like a meadow—fun and pretty, and nice—doesn't mean it's not just a swamp. But you have to see it for yourself to be sure."

I hadn't thought of the story like that before. I had always just had it in my head as a funny story of us being stupid, but seeing it in this light was interesting. I hadn't thought, before, about how my own stories could "teach" me anything at all.

"Ooh. Nice moral."

"Why thank you," I said, bowing dramatically. "Now it's your turn."

Billy did a few neck rolls, his chin to his chest, then

tilted his chin violently to the left, resulting in a crack that sounded like a snapping branch.

"Okay. When I was in high school, I ran away from home."

I contorted my face into an appropriate level of confusion and concern. He tried a few times to crack the other side of his neck, then gave up and massaged it instead.

"Basically, I thought I had the worst life on earth. My grandma basically raised me, and she was sweet but strict. I was never allowed to do—well, anything, really, but she especially hated loud noises. So even if I was allowed to have friends over, we couldn't laugh too loud. But we also weren't allowed to go outside, because she was afraid of the neighborhood.

"Worst of all was the drums. I begged her to buy me drums. I was in love with them—we did them a bit in music class in school, and my teacher said I had a real knack for it. I don't think I'd ever been told I had a 'knack' for anything before. I started listening to all these punk bands with killer drum lines. I was playing along with pencils, quietly on my mattress. She finally bought me some drums—a beautiful set, but she wouldn't let me play them with the sticks. They were too loud. She let me play only with the brushes. I was trying to play all this heavy stuff, sounding like a smooth jazz musician who got lost at Riot Fest.

"So, the day that was the breaking point, I came home from somewhere and it was maybe eight. I walked in the door and my grandmother looked at me with honest-to-god fear in her eyes and said, 'You're not gonna go play those drums, are you?' And I said, you know, not thinking, I said,

'No, I don't feel like it.' And she tossed her hands up in the air and said, 'Hallelujah!' and then laughed as she stirred a thing of soup.

"She was joking, obviously, but I was still like, 'Seriously?' Then she came over and hugged me, and I just felt so suffocated and—like I said—I just felt like no one in the world had it worse than me. I mean, I knew kids were starving in Africa and whatever, and Grandma never beat me or anything, but no one 'in my situation' had it worse than me, I figured.

"So, I packed up my drums and my clothes and ran away. Made it all the way to the city where I learned that, yes, in fact, other people 'in my situation' had it worse than me. Soon, I became one of those people who 'had it worse.' And after a few years, I found myself running away again. Of course, this time I had some help, but that's a different story."

He gazed off at the floor. "I'm a double runaway. Never saw my grandma or my city friends again once I left them. Never made it big playing drums, either. But, as they say, third time's the charm. Now I have a girlfriend who loves me unconditionally and who plays bass with me, and I can be on the drums as loud as we want."

We sat in a warm silence.

"So," I finally piped up, tucking what remained of my snack back in my bag, "what did you learn?"

"I learned to never give up," he said quickly, like he'd had it prepared. "A good life is out there for everyone. And I learned someone always has it worse than you do, unimaginably worse. Or rather, it's unimaginable until you also get in that situation."

Ha! He *does* agree with me. "So, to always be grateful, right?"

He thought a moment. "No, I don't think 'always' or 'grateful' are quite right. More like, 'have empathy, as often as is healthy for your individual mental health.'" He thought again, then added, "For yourself, and others."

I smirked. "That doesn't quite fit on a yoga T-shirt, though."

"Dammit. My profitability, no!" We laughed. "Oh—I also learned that sometimes risks are worth it. Like with you and Elise. Good luck tonight."

Twelve

How to Get on the Naughty List

Originally, our second date was going to be at Elise's apartment, but one of her roommates had a big exam (apparently in college, tests are called "exams") the next day, and asked for the apartment to be quiet so she could get a good night's rest. That was fine with me. I was hella nervous about being in someone's apartment that they, themselves, paid money to live in. It seemed so grown up.

Anyway, Elise texted me the morning of and told me the situation with palpable disappointment. She really wanted to cook a killer vegetarian dinner for me, she said with a winky face that I stared at for far longer than was strictly necessary. We decided we'd do that next time (a third date seemed like a more appropriate date in which to "go home with a girl," anyway), and this time Elise and I were supposed to just see a movie in theaters.

It was supposed to be this dark, historical drama, but after such a real conversation with Billy, my serious emotions needed a break. So, when Elise finally left Pandora's Box, I looped my arm in hers and pulled her up to my speed. Her blazer flapped against my side.

"Hey!" she said with a laugh, holding chunky dreads away from her eyes.

"Let's skip the movie," I said, trying with all my might to weave in the sparkly air of adventure found in every teen romance. "Wanna go do something illegal?"

Her eyes lit up behind her glasses. "Yes! Wait, what exactly?"

I slid my hand down to grab her by the wrist and broke off into a run through the mall corridor, past the pet shop with rabbits in the window, past MakeAlive Cosmetics, past the diamond place, and down the hallway with dad's security office. I pulled her back into the service hallway. Employees were only really allowed in the hallways that led to their stores, and I was only technically allowed back here to get to Max's office, but thanks to hide and seek with Claire, John, and Nora (and various tours from my dad), I knew the place inside and out.

She was keeping up now, right behind my elbow, so I let go of her wrist. "Mo! I don't wanna get fired—"

"Don't worry," I said. "This is just a shortcut."

"A shortcut to mall jail?" She said it as a joke, but I could hear the twinge of serious worry in her voice.

I didn't have a plan, but when I saw that ashy mark on the floor where I'd put out my first cigarette, I thought of one and sped past cardboard boxes and unpainted doors to veer right into Max's office. Far from illegal on my end, but the night was young.

I let us in after a big show of listening at the door.

"Oh, no way!" She beamed once I flicked on the light. "Is this Santa's stuff?"

She ran past Billy's jacket and Max's desk to the dusty Santa stuff. She ran her hands over his fluffy red coat. It was kind of weird to see her in this room. There were still some panini crumbs on the desk from earlier.

"Isn't it neat?" I said, trying to work out how to make it seem like coming here was some big romantic plan.

"Um, *yeah*, dude. Everyone sat with Santa as a kid, but who—" she took the coat off the hanger, working it around the pants that hung beneath, "—ever gets to wear his coat? Or his hat?" She grabbed his hat off the rack and pulled it down low so the fuzz peeked in under her glasses.

"Only very good little boys and girls," I said in a deep, jolly Santa approximation.

I took a wide-legged seat on Santa's big red armchair— after scooping a few armfuls of files onto the floor beside it. I stroked an imaginary beard. I had to sit right on the edge of the chair for my feet to hit the ground.

Elise stepped around and over various props, arms out and balancing like she was walking through a rocky stream.

"So, what would you like for Christmas?" I held out my hand to her, and she took it with a little bow of her head.

She gestured down at her jacket. "I thought *I* was Santa?"

"Sorry, little girl. Nice cosplay, though."

Elise smirked and took that opportunity to sit sideways on my lap, fawning over me, her arms around my shoulders and her foot rising up my leg, overly sexy. Not Santa-appropriate at *all*.

"Well, then, tell me, Santa: have I been a *good girl* this year?"

I cracked into laughter, and Elise did, too.

"Oh, my god," I managed, trying to get a hold of my laughter.

"I—I told you I was bad at flirting!"

The realization that she was being serious—that it wasn't a goofy, ironic joke—sent me off again.

"Holy crap," I finally said. "Okay, maybe you're not the most subtle flirter."

"I wear my heart on my sleeve," she said, bright pink with joy and good-natured embarrassment. God, blush looked good on her.

"You're not a great flirter," I said, becoming more serious now. "But you are…" my fingers on her chin, taking a page from her own book. "A great…" She's serious now too, a smile playing at perfect lips, eyes half closed. Billy's right—it's easier to act than talk. I don't care. We're here now, and— "Kisser."

I tilted my head just a bit and we were kissing. We kissed for a long time on Santa's chair. I pulled her close. She turned on my lap to straddle me (holy shit) and I ran my hands up her neck with the intention of running into her hair—that's when I was reminded of her Santa hat and had to break off to laugh again.

"Dang, Santa, you're a good kisser," she said.

"That's not you flirting again, is it? That was a joke?" I teased.

"Yes, that was a joke! Obviously!"

"Okay, well, it's hard to tell with you some—"

She kissed me again, passionately, deeply.

"That shut you up," she whispered, smiling.

"You ought to keep that trick in mind."

We made out on Santa's chair for what felt like hours but was actually only a few minutes. But then I started worrying about getting caught, specifically since Max would probably be the one escorting Billy back at the end of the shift, so I told Elise it was time for part two of our night of doing illegal things.

Of course, I was still improvising, mind whirring as I put the files back and Elise took off the Santa gear, but the gleam in her eye took my worries away.

I had some weed in my car, but smoking wasn't exactly innovative—or illegal, anymore. Besides, she offered to pack a bowl while I drove, so I knew this wasn't anything new for her.

She packed, I drove, a good song played on the radio, all was chill.

I was daydreaming about shoplifting together. She could fuck Pandora's Box from the inside out (so to speak). Actually, we could make a fortune.

The thought weirdly made me sick to my stomach. Not because I felt bad about the stealing—I repeat, victimless crime—but because profiting off it felt like overkill. I never sold what I stole. I didn't know how—Mom's lessons never got that far in the process. Besides, I had no idea whether or not Elise would be cool with stealing. Even *Billy* wasn't cool with it, and the dude was in a gang. Well. I was ninety percent sure he had been in a gang, at some point.

I decided to test the waters at the 7-Eleven nearest my high school. They were remarkably easy to steal from.

I slammed the car in park and it whined out a protest—old, sad thing.

"Can you guess why we're here?" I asked as we headed in through the doors, setting off an electric chime.

Elise looked around animatedly, hand over her eyes like a sailor. "Hmmm…" Then she darted to the freezer and pulled out a carton of eggs. "We're going to egg somebody's house?"

Damn, she was so cute and so excited. So, *into* anything. She'd already made too much of a memorable scene for me to feel comfortable shoplifting anyway…

And hell, Nora deserved it.

"You are so smart," I said, wrinkling my nose and snatching the eggs from her hands. She tossed her hair and thanked me in a posh accent. I paid for the eggs.

I didn't even know 7-Eleven sold eggs.

Thirteen

The Time We Egged a House

I asked if Elise had anyone she wanted to egg. She said she did, an ex-boyfriend, but he lived a state away now.

"It should be somebody who deserves it. We shouldn't hurt anyone innocent," Elise said, packing another bowl. "We could egg the guy who protested the cannabis shop."

"Well…I've got somebody."

"An ex-girlfriend?"

"More like ex-*friend*, full stop."

I had said that for the word play, but it hurt when I heard the words coming out of my mouth. Was she really my "ex" friend?

Nora's place was decent. Kind of similar to mine—the kind of house that implied the owners would have lived in a studio apartment if this was a city. It was an A-frame with a never-used rocking chair on the front porch. All the lights were off, and her mom's car was gone, but Nora's shitty sedan and her dad's van were in the driveway. It was just past eight and passing from twilight into true darkness. I knew her family ate dinner kind of late, so I figured they must have been all out to eat. I couldn't have planned it any better.

"This is it," I said, slamming the car in park, turning off

the radio but leaving the engine running. My car was half up on the curb and we could *probably* have thrown the eggs from there, but Elise reached for the door so I got out, too. She handed me an egg, stifling giggles. I checked the windows of the houses nearby. Some lights on, but no faces nearby.

I rolled the egg around my palm. I knew Nora's room—the one with the AC unit sticking out the window on the left side of the house. If I hit that unit, I figured, her room would smell like rotten eggs for weeks. Or maybe it would just sit there, dripping into the unit unnoticed until she turned it on for the first time in a couple months and then threw up from the smell. I could see her gagging now, on her hands and knees on her garish orange carpet. She'd choke, leaning against her bed, right under that kiddie mobile of planes and balloons she—for some reason—still has on the ceiling.

Yeah. I rolled my shoulders back. *Yeah.*

"So," Elise said, a chipper, sexy darkness in her voice. "What'd this bitch do to you?"

I thought. I chuckled. Nothing, really, except make me feel awful.

"My mom died five years ago," I said. Elise started to react with sympathy, so I waved my hand. "It's fine. I mean, I'm not in grief all the time, or anything, but…I mean, my mom died. And all *Nora* does all day…all she does is complain about her parents."

"Oh, gotcha," Elise said. I glanced over—it seemed like she was still in the process of getting it, actually. "Still…so sorry to hear about your mom."

She took my hand. I smiled and ran my thumb over her fingers, stopping when I reached a bandage wrapped around her fingernail.

"So, Nora?" she said after a minute.

"Nora...I just don't have patience for her—for her complaining about her mom. Because her mom is alive. *My* mom is dead. You know? And sure, she wasn't a great mom. I—"

I saw Mom then in the back of my mind, drugged out of her skull, in nothing but a sports bra and sweatpants on the couch, eyes dazed up at the ceiling. I saw her, undressing me in the mall bathroom, praising me for stealing two bras at once. I saw her, dead in the hospital room—

"She was actually a terrible mom, and I had a lot to complain about. But I would give anything to—to have her yell at me again. And this bitch Nora—"

I shook my head. My words clogged up behind my tongue.

"There's some other stuff, too," I began, but my voice stopped working after that. All the Nora bullshit was stoppered up like cotton in my mouth.

I took my right hand out of Elise's, grabbed the egg, wound up, and threw it like a cannonball at the siding of Nora's house. It fell too quickly and splattered on the cement of the foundation.

Elise considered the egg in her hand, spinning it in her palm with her bandaged fingers. My shattered egg slunk, sunk, then plopped onto the grass with a rustle.

"This was stupid, I—"

"You need this, huh?" Elise whispered, looking up at

me from the corner of her eye. "She really did something to hurt you, didn't she?"

"I—"

An egg smashed into the back bumper of Nora's dad's van.

"Oh, shit," Elise said, blocking her mouth with her free hand. "I was aiming for the house!"

Joy illuminated my chest. I grabbed two eggs in each hand and pinwheeled my arm into a throw to make Elise laugh. We whipped those eggs everywhere—the shutters, the front bushes, the back windshield of Nora's car. My prize shot was my last: a hearty smack against the front door.

I ran and jumped in the car, laughing but now paranoid of the noise we had made. Just as I buckled in, a light went on upstairs, in Nora's room. *Shit shit shit.*

"Get in, get in!" I whisper-shouted.

Elise had one more egg and nailed the mailbox on her way around to the passenger's side.

I hit the gas and we were gone. The radio blasted, the windows down, both of us laughing so hard we couldn't breathe. I got on the highway, trying to get as far away as fast as possible. Highway driving still made me nervous, but I tried not to show it.

After a very stressful merge, Elise sighed and said to the stars, "That was so fun."

"It was!"

"Looked cathartic for you."

"It was."

"That's good. I could tell it was...important."

We drove in silence a moment more. I was thinking about how Claire and John would never egg Nora's house with me. If they were here, we'd be egging the guy who protested the cannabis shop. Elise understood me more than they did, and I hadn't even known her for a week.

"So, about that girl..."

"Nora?"

"You don't have to tell me. I just...it seems like there was more to the story there than what you said, about her complaining about her parents." Before I could work out a response, she continued, "I kind of feel like you regret the things you *don't* say more than the things you do say, you know? And I could help, if I knew—but if you'd rather just ride and tell me later, we can do that, too."

Her head was turned to the road, but I could feel her eyes on me. My heart was pounding.

"Let's do that," I said, kindly, and she went back to smiling at the stars.

I was reeling. I'd already *told* Elise what Nora "did" to me, and she doesn't think it was bad enough to warrant an egging. I was angry at Nora for overreacting, and now Elise thinks *I'm* overreacting. Actually, she thinks I'm not overreacting, but hiding something worse Nora did, because no one in their right mind would think a little complaining would warrant getting egged.

But that's actually all she did. At that time. That's what I was thinking about. *Was* I overreacting?

I tightened my grip on the steering wheel. The mall's parking lot, lit up by a thousand streetlamps, came into view, and I thought about you. You, my therapist, and how you listen so intently with a concerned, turned-in look on your face, and how you act like my pain is "valid" and "earned" even when you must get a dozen people who are way worse off than me coming through your door every day.

And I always felt like you were lying. Because how the fuck am I deserving of your time?

Fourteen

No Thanks, Brain

So, you know this part already. Duh, you were there. But it really did impact me—the therapy session we had soon after the egging.

I told you what we did, since I now knew you couldn't tell anybody. I kept watching your reaction, trying to gauge how you felt about it.

You nodded, made a note. Sorry, but it's a little irritating how little feedback you give sometimes.

"Why do you think Nora doesn't have a right to complain about her parents?"

"Because—" I could hear the words I was about to say in my head, about how my mom's dead and hers is alive, and it did sound pretty childish. I said it anyway, then quickly followed up with, "I mean, my *mom* is *dead*. I have justification. She doesn't."

"Do you think it could be possible you don't know the whole story?"

"Obviously," I said, getting a little heated. "I know I don't, 'cause she won't *tell* us the whole story."

You smiled a little. "Welcome to my world."

I smiled a little back, despite myself. "But I don't know, I told Elise the whole story about our fight. *My* side of the whole story. And she didn't seem to think it was bad enough, right? It's the same situation," I realized, "in reverse. I thought Nora's problem wasn't bad enough to complain about, and now Elise thinks my problem with Nora isn't bad enough to...egg her house. And she made me wonder, maybe it's not. Maybe she didn't deserve it? But maybe, then, her parents don't deserve to be complained about." I was confusing myself. "So, I'm back at square one."

"That's an interesting word, 'deserve,'" you said. "It implies that someone is a judge. Some outside source decides what is deserving of...sympathy, of punishment, of your emotions."

I didn't really get where you were going with that. Elise had said "deserve" last night, when we were trying to decide whose house to egg. "Yeah..."

"You know how I know every one of my clients 'deserves' therapy? Even the ones who don't have obvious or—shall we say—dire problems?"

"I know therapy isn't only for crazy people. I'm here, and I don't think I'm crazy." I tossed my hair sarcastically. "*I* only have five out of the top seven signs of depression, after all."

"I don't think you're crazy either," you said. "But that's exactly it. I don't believe you even need five-out-of-seven-signs-of-*whatever* to benefit from therapy. I believe you don't need any symptoms of anything at all to benefit from a therapist."

Of course not, I thought. *You're a therapist.*

"But you have to admit, some people need it *more* than others," I said. "I think I probably need it less than others."

"Well, like I said, I believe *everyone* can benefit from a therapist," you continued. "Because I believe everyone's life—everyone's—has challenges too big for one person to deal with on their own."

Claire had basically said the same thing. I let that one sink in for a while, just sitting and picking at the fabric on my car-key lanyard. I realized my shoulders were hunched up all tense, so I lowered them. A wave of relief flooded down the muscles in my back.

"I actually agree with that," I finally said. "On one level. But part of me just can't believe it." I paused, thought. "It's like when you think about how you're gonna die one day, and you know it's true. Nothing's ever not died before. But a small part of you doesn't believe it. Or—" I laughed. "Or when you're ten and you pretend you still believe in the Easter Bunny because you're afraid if you admit otherwise, you'll stop getting chocolate."

You nodded, a slight smile on your lips. "It's hard to rewrite old beliefs."

You paused for me to go on, but I didn't have much else to say. I checked the clock—I was sad we only had ten minutes left.

"I want you to try something this week," you said then. "Pay attention to those thoughts—from both the negative and positive 'sides' of you. Those different 'parts' of you, different voices. The one who says you deserve therapy, and the one who says you don't." I made a face, and you held up your palms like, *whoa*. "I'm not asking you to pick one over the other, or anything. Just pay attention to them, and work on realizing that you have control over them. You might have heard the phrase 'You are not your thoughts'?" I shook my head. "Well, you're not your thoughts. You get to choose which thoughts you believe—that part that still believes in immortality, or the part that doesn't. The part that believes some people don't have enough suffering in their life to warrant a complaint, and the part that believes everybody needs help, sometimes. Listen to all the parts, then decide which one you want to listen to most."

Sounds weird, I thought immediately. And then, for the first time I tried doing what you said. Part of me thinks that this sounds weird, yes. But another part thought it sounded helpful. So, I decided to find it helpful and not listen to the negative voice. But it was hard to shut it up completely.

"Isn't that basically just lying to yourself?"

"Well. Let's say you're hearing me say this, and your mind says, 'that's stupid.'" (You were nearly spot-on. That wasn't the only time I thought you might be reading my mind, by the way.) "You can either believe that thought, or not. You can realize that a part of your mind—everyone's mind, not just yours—resists anything that's strange and unfamiliar. It does this to protect us. But we have the power to say, 'Thank you, Brain, but I'm going to follow a different thought today. I'm going to stay open and accepting instead of following my first judgment.'"

"That sounds good," I said quietly, thinking over in my head how many of those judgments I had and submitted to every day. "But hard."

"It *is* hard. It takes time. And everyone messes up at it, even 'experts' like me." You did the finger quotes. I liked that. "I'm just asking you to try. How does that sound?"

You probably give this advice to a lot of your clients. I hope you do. It's great advice. And even though you only gave it to me like three weeks ago, it changed my life. It might've saved my life, actually. But I'm getting ahead of myself, again.

"I'll *try* it, anyway," I said. And I decided to believe myself.

Fifteen

Forgive and Forget

Dad stopped by my work. I didn't see him coming—no one was in line, so I was reading for English class. He sauntered on up and drummed his fingers on the page. I jumped.

"Hard at work?" he said, smiling.

"Hey, Dad."

"How's it going?"

"Good. Cool. You know." I smiled. "Want a picture?" I added, joking.

"Nah, nah. Hey, is that for school?" He pointed at my book.

"Yeah."

"You keeping those grades up? Progress report in two weeks."

"Yep."

"Good, good. Hoping things are…" He made some weird gestures—a thumbs-up, then pointing up, then kind of vaguely gesturing at my head. "You know, with the…" He pointed at the exit, in the general direction of your office. "That lady you're talking to?"

"Yeah." I realized I had an opportunity here. I lowered my voice just a touch. "Hey, Dad…I saw you the other day, talking to some guys with tattoos up there." I nodded at the second floor.

"Mm." He squinted up at the top of the escalators. "Remember when you were interviewing, and I told you about the sketchy characters we've seen hanging around?"

I swallowed. "Yeah."

"Yeah. Harmless so far, but my gang radar isn't usually wrong." He lowered his eyebrows. "Be careful, okay?"

"I will."

"Good." He tapped the desk. "Good! Well, I'll...let you get back to it."

"Cool, thanks. See ya."

He left. Once he was out of sight, I buried my face in the palm of my hand. *God.* Why was talking to my dad like bumping into an ex from elementary school?

"You know," I said to Billy at the beginning of our next break. "I always kinda knew you were supposed to learn stuff from books, but I'd never put it into words that we learn, like, 'Aesop fables' lessons from real life, too."

Billy smiled as he lit his cigarette, blowing the smoke out the side of his mouth.

"I mean, I know getting stung by a bee teaches you not to mess with bees," I clarified when he didn't reply. "But to work out what you learned from something bigger—like the meadow story—I just feel like it's a cool way to go about it."

"For sure," he said, brightening into a—not quite a smile, but that kind of wide-eyed joy of intellectual stimulation. "My therapist turned me on to it like a year ago. She said it was the only way to forgive and forget."

Forgive and forget. Jeez. I figured if I had Billy's therapist she'd've said I'd have to forgive and forget what Nora said. Or even forgive and forget all the times my mom was a shitty mom.

"It sucks that the person who gets hurt always has to be the one doing the forgiving," I said. "And forgetting."

I was kind of lost in my thoughts, saying high thoughts without even being high. But then Billy sat up with really intense energy, the soles of his shoes slapping on the ground.

"Yes! Okay. When I was selling drugs in the city—"

"Wait, what?"

I *knew* this dude sold drugs.

He paused, looked around at the junk on the desk, shrugged, tried to be all nonchalant. "Well, I wasn't only playing drums. Had to pay rent somehow."

I laughed a little. "Okay, cool." I didn't know, really, how to react. I didn't mind, I guess. Maybe I should have.

He shrugged again. "Anyway, one of my buddies, Thomas, and I; we were killing it with—ah, I think they had just put me in Cambridge for a start. Lots of college kids and—well, whatever. One of my roommates—we were living with six or seven guys at this point—he asked out Mariah, who was also a dealer—and about twenty-seven, okay? And I was fifteen or sixteen. Didn't matter. I loved her, and I was devastated when they started dating. I never really got over it. It's the only bad thing that dude ever did to me, but even now when I think of him it's the first thought that comes to my mind—how much he sucks for taking Mariah off the market. I brought him up to my therapist and she says—" he cleared an imaginary table of clutter with a sweep of his hands. "—'Forgive and forget.' And I say, 'How?' So she says, 'Write out your story about what happened, to start.' So, I did, and brought it back the next week. Then she goes, 'What did you learn from that story?'"

He paused, relit the cigarette that had somehow died out.

"And?" I cut in. "What did you learn?"

"I wasn't sure, at the time. But then I thought about it like I was reading a story. And I think I learned that it makes no sense to hold a grudge. Me being mad at him didn't do a thing to him then, and it does even less now. So, now I know that. But I still don't know *how* to get over it, though. You know? I can tell myself a hundred times to get over it, but whenever I think of him, I feel this flash of rage before I can even think of anything else." He took a deep sigh. "But, that's why I'm still in therapy, I guess."

"That's wild," I said. "I was just talking to my therapist yesterday about how hard it is to listen to your positive and negative thoughts, and choose to follow the good ones. And I said, like, 'I don't know how to believe something if I don't, you know, already believe it.' She said it basically takes practice."

We nodded together for a while, letting it fill the air like his smoke.

"I guess that counts for my story…?"

I grinned. Then I told him the softball story, *with* the Mom part.

The softball story on its surface is just what I told you during our first session—I was so bad at softball I ran the wrong way around the bases. The Mom part is…well, you have to know, first of all, that she was sitting on the left side of the field. And I didn't see her come in. I don't know where she was, or how she got there, but she wasn't supposed to be there that day. So, when she showed up, I was so excited. There she was, cheering and waving at me from the sidelines, clutching an iced coffee in one hand.

"Yes! Go Maureen!"

I can still hear her voice.

I smiled at her, blushing hot deep into my chest. I was up. The ball came—the pressure was on. Mom finally came to a game! I drove all my weight into that little bat and it cracked like Fenway. The thing went soaring, seriously.

And I was pumped. I wanted to run so Mom could see me. I took off to the left, and I see her pointing the other way. *Go for second?* I beamed and hit second. Now she's laughing, shouting, "Mo!" or maybe "Go?" (I found out later it was "No.") Everyone was pointing at home. I ran—sped past the third base. I couldn't believe it—I was going to make a home run with Mom watching! I got back to home and threw my little arms in the air above my head.

A home run!

I did what all the other little girls did and ran back, around, and up the bleachers to my mom and dad. I hugged . her first, breathless.

"Oh, Maureen," Mom said, laughing so hard she was

nearly as out of breath as I was. At first, I thought she was overwhelmed with joy, but then I heard Coach say, "Aisha's still looking for the ball, so…she would have made it. We're going to count it."

"Count it?" I said, catching Dad's eye, knowing he'd explain. *Why wouldn't they count it?*

Dad opened his mouth, but then Mom burst out, "You went the wrong way around the bases!"

She was laughing at me. And I felt it.

"I only ran that way to impress her," I said to Billy. "I wanted her to see me run, so I ran on the side of the field she was on."

"And what did that teach you?"

"To quit softball."

Billy raised his eyebrows. I took a deep, dramatic breath and thought for a minute.

"It taught me to not get flustered and worried about what my—well, what anybody thinks. And, that everyone has a better time if you can learn to laugh at yourself. Because when I started crying everyone stopped having such a good time."

And those are good enough morals. But I don't know if either lesson really sunk in too well.

Mostly I learned that Mom would laugh at my mistakes, but Dad wouldn't.

"Anyway." I rocked to my feet. "Yeah. You got your karma points for today. Few more weeks with me and you'll be back to net zero." I widened my eyes at the desktop, wishing I was in bed already. "Woo."

He threw out his trash, and stared in the bin for a while.

He met my eyes, throat tight, like he was maybe about to break into tears.

"I hope…this is helping. That it's not completely selfish. I didn't mean it to be."

His voice was so soft, my heart ached. I nodded. "It is. It's not selfish."

He put on the mask, and then the dead-eyed, muffled bunny said, "Sometimes, I'm not sure if there's anything in the world a person can do that isn't somehow selfish."

Sixteen

Changing Focus

The next day on set, Elise was supposed to bring her niece by for a bunny photo. And, obviously, it couldn't just go *well*. Nothing's ever easy.

It's stupid. The mall is pretty big—you've probably been there, you know. And my dad is usually busy. Otherwise, my friends and I would never hang out at the mall. But of course, today he decided to swing by.

I must have sent him too many welcoming vibes the day before.

He waved to me as he approached, from twenty feet behind the line area (no one was in line). I was running the cash register, doing homework again. I gave a little wave. Shit. I was already anxious that Elise was on her way. I didn't want to have to pretend in front of Dad, too.

"Hey, kiddo." He leaned his elbow on the desk.

"Hey."

"Just busted a shoplifter out of that kitchen store by Macy's."

Amateur. "Oh, yeah?"

"Yeah, you know. Young kid, showing off for his friends. Gave him a warning."

"Oh, yeah, cool." More for me. I felt kind of weird,

suddenly having my dad talk to me about shoplifting. It was making me paranoid, and it was all too much, on top of waiting for Elise. "Hey, um...I'm not really supposed to talk to people while I'm—"

"Hey, Max!" Dad called.

I heard Max turn away from the camera. "Oh, hey, Gerald. Good day?"

"Great day, great day, and you?"

I *craved* death.

"Good, good. Kind of slow, but. You know."

"Good, yeah, good." Then Dad turned back to me. "So, I was just wondering if you've got anything going on after work today."

"Oh, I—"

Then Elise came into view, because God hates me. She had a little girl by the hand and was hunching down so the girl could hear her better as they walked. They were both pretty cute. Her niece looked to be about four and was wearing a pink shirt with a cartoon bunny on the tummy, a green tutu over purple pants, and had some sort of sparkly sticker on her face—but even with all that, Elise was even cuter. Her dreads were piled up in a clumsy, messy bun and she was wearing a jean jacket littered with patches of skulls and roses, and I think the logo for Amnesty International.

"Yeah, I'm busy," I said. "Sorry."

"Oh, no, not a big deal. I just heard that Chinese place you like is doing a special. Free appetizers for law enforcement, and your dad still has his old badge, so—"

"Aw. Another time."

"Sure, yeah."

He straightened and rolled his shoulders back, squinting off into the distance. *Come on come on come on come on just leaveleaveleaveleaveleave*—I held strong, not saying a single word. I flipped the page in my math book, even though I didn't have to.

"Well, I better mosey on," he said, finally. Elise was within earshot by now. "Let me know when you've got a day off, yeah?"

"Okay. See ya."

"See ya round."

He winked, and as he left, he passed Elise. She took a few steps past him and scanned the set. When she saw me, she waved. I waved back. Dad had just started climbing up the broken up-escalator and turned around and, thinking I was waving at him, waved at me again while he said something into his walkie talkie. Oh, *God*. It was like a sitcom.

I shut my math book, gritted my teeth, and pretended to punch some important buttons on the register while Elise and her niece made their way through the winding, pink velvet rope barriers. The line really was, sometimes, that long, but usually not. Right then, it was completely empty.

After zooming around two corners, Elise said, "Hey, watch this!"

I looked up in time to see her duck under the remaining three lines of velvet rope. The little girl's face lit up and she plodded after Elise, picking up the rope over her head like Elise did, even though she could fit underneath it fine.

As they approached, Dad reached the top of the broken

escalator, still talking on his walkie talkie, and disappeared down the hall.

Phew. So maybe God doesn't hate me so much, after all.

"Hi!" I said to Elise and her niece, very high-pitched and excited. "Welcome, welcome, who do we have here?"

I brought them in toward the set. Max must have heard the shift in my tone. He looked back at me from the camera with bemused, twisted lips.

"This is Brayden," Elise said, landing her hands on Brayden's shoulders and pulling her gently back against her knees. Brayden smiled up at me, tucking her chin cutely into her chest. Now I could see the sticker on her face was actually a temporary tattoo of a rainbow.

"I love your tattoo," I said.

"It's a rainbow!"

"Gotta start 'em young," Elise deadpanned. I bit my cheek to stifle a smile.

Brayden was, I admit, pretty adorable in her poofy nylon tutu. She was staring, starstruck, at Billy, her sleeve in her mouth, getting soaked with spit.

"Brayden, Mommy doesn't want you doing that, remember?" Elise eased Brayden's hand gently away from her mouth, then looked up to me with a knowing eye roll. "My twin sister's a—" she mouthed the word "bitch," then said out loud, "—strict mother."

Twin?

"I didn't know you had a twin."

"Mm. Identical in everything except personality and

life choices. And she stole two of my wisdom teeth in the womb. Serves her right."

I was pretty dazed by all that. I didn't even know tooth stealing could happen. I wasn't sure it could. I'm still not sure, actually.

I'd never seen Elise so un-collected. She was usually so composed, but Brayden was making her kind of zoned out. Elise told me when we met that she "just" turned twenty. And if Brayden was three or four, that meant her sister must have given birth around sixteen or seventeen, and Elise must have gone through all that right along with her. I wondered what all that was like, for Elise and especially for her sister. I was thankful I'd never have to deal with a pregnancy like that.

There have been two girls in my year that have gotten pregnant, that I'm aware of. Not too many, considering what I saw in the high school in Somerville. One got an abortion, and the other one actually went through with it. It was wild, because I kept thinking, *Oh, poor Helena, she's gonna be pregnant.* And then she had the baby, and really only then it hit me that, oh, shit—Helena is a *mom.* And now she has a *baby.* And in a couple years, her baby won't be a baby anymore, because they'll be Brayden's age. And I'll probably be in college, smoking weed and procrastinating finals, and Helena will be watching *The Little Mermaid* for the fortieth time with a three-year-old. That's wild. That's weird.

I had so much I wanted to ask Elise. I wanted to meet her sister. I wanted to know if she was still with her boyfriend—or, whoever Brayden's father was. I wanted to know how Elise felt about the whole thing. She seemed like she was a fun aunt, but she also seemed super stressed just by having the kid around. But I didn't have time to ask anything. I had to walk them to the bunny, so I just focused on my job.

There was one thing I had to say, though.

"Hey, so, that guy who just left is my dad, and—"

"*He's* your dad? The security guy? I see him all the time; I had no idea!"

That was weird. I felt like she knew me so well already, but she didn't know my dad worked at the mall, which was pretty much the thing that *everyone* knows about me. Then again, I didn't know she was a twin.

"Yeah...um, I'm not exactly 'out' to him yet, and so—"

"Oh, gotcha. Damn," she said, in sympathy, I think. "Okay. Well. I won't ask to be introduced, then." She smiled.

"Thanks for understanding."

"Of course, babe," she said. My breath caught in my throat. That was the first time she'd called me "babe," or any pet name. But then she added, "I mean, of course, Friend-o," with an exaggerated wink, and I realized it was part of a joke.

I let Elise come stand closer, just a couple feet behind Max and the camera. I wanted to kiss her, but didn't know if my dad would reappear so I didn't risk it. Plus, Max might tell my dad, or otherwise let it slip, and I couldn't let that happen.

"Wait here," I said. I jogged over to Max. "Hey, mind if I take this pic for my friend?"

Max took a glance at Elise, who gave a closed-mouth smile. "Knock yourself out," Max said. "I'll do cash for a bit."

Max was a pretty good boss. I think. In my limited experience.

I waved Elise and Brayden over, and Brayden hesitantly tip-toed closer to Billy, only letting go of Elise's hand when Elise whispered it was all okay. Billy waved, trying to appear friendly, but something adults often lose sight of is how unironically creepy a six-foot, silent bunny with dead eyes can be, especially when you're hardly half their size.

"Show me how you do it?"

Elise was being cute, hands clasped behind her back.

"Well. It's pretty high-tech stuff, I'm not sure if you'll understand, but...try to keep up."

"I'll do my best."

"So. First, I wait for the kids to get settled on the bunny's lap. Then—you paying attention? This is hard stuff."

"Wait, you already lost me."

I bumped my shoulder into hers, and she bumped me one back.

"Then I lean down like this—" I put my eye to the camera. "Then I say, 'Brayden!'" Brayden looked up at the camera, biting at her sleeve again. "Saaaaaay...'Cheese-ter bunny!'"

Brayden giggle-shouted, "Cheese-ter bunny!" and I snapped the pic. It looked awesome. Photogenic little kiddo.

Elise squeezed my hand, just subtle enough that should

a dad be watching, he wouldn't question it. "You're a pro. I could never be so skilled."

"I know, babe, you're so lucky."

I called her "babe" to see how it felt, not as part of a joke. It felt nice. Intimate, kind of. Brayden grabbed a chocolate and high-fived Billy, then high-tenned Billy when he held out another big bunny hand.

Elise smiled, squeezed my hand once more. "I feel lucky," she said quietly.

"Really?"

"Really really."

"Well, me too."

"Well, you should."

"Oh, should I?"

"Yup."

I couldn't resist it. I gave her a quick kiss then walked them both up to Max at the counter, checking the second floor. No dad. Max didn't see. I really did feel lucky.

Elise bought the second-cheapest package for Brayden's mom, had Brayden give me a hug, and then they left.

It was so, so, so nice. I felt giddy the rest of the day.

I suppose that wasn't a super significant moment, but I only had so many moments with Elise before I totally blew it, so they all kind of feel important, even if, I guess, they're not.

But if I were telling this story to Billy, I'd say I learned that little moments of joy can make a whole day brighter. And that if I focused on how much I really liked Elise, my day would have been a lot more peaceful than what I chose to do, which was to focus on how chicken I am when it comes to coming out to my dad, and when my brain got tired of that it started whipping up scenarios of what it must have been like for Elise's twin to have a baby in high school, and what it must have been like for Elise to have watched her sister go through all that.

So, I guess really what I learned is that you were right—I focus on the negative, like, all the time.

Seventeen

Masks

I was still in a cyclone of negativity when I walked Billy back to break. I tried to do what you asked me to do and tell myself, "Thank you, brain, but I'm going to focus on something else now." I tried that, and it kind of worked for a couple minutes, but after a while my brain would whisper, "Dad will probably tell you it's a phase," like it was something I didn't want to forget to pick up at the store on my way home.

So, I don't know how well I did at that. But maybe just trying is…something?

"You look lost in thought, Ladybug."

"Thinking about Elise," I lied, but then suddenly it was the truth. "That was her, today."

"Who?!"

I paused. Didn't he notice I kissed her? "With the dreadlocks? I showed her the camera—"

"Oh…vaguely, I remember her. Shoot, I wish I knew that was *her* her."

"No worries," I said with a smile, still fighting my brain, still trying to keep thinking about something nice.

I figured a "nice" distraction would help, so I said, "Hey, for today, why don't you tell me how you got your tattoos?" because I figured there was probably some positivity there.

But Billy sucked in air like he was trying to squeeze me into his busy weekend, tilting his head side to side a couple times.

"You don't have to," I added in my best nonchalant voice, but he waved a dismissive hand and said, "Nah, fuck it. It's just not a great story."

That's when I realized how dumb the idea was. I had just discovered the dude was in a *gang* and *sold drugs*. Well, I guess I wasn't sure if he was in a gang, but he definitely did sell drugs, and he definitely did hang out with those guys, some of whom had similar-looking tattoos, so I didn't think the "gang" theory was too far off. It wasn't going to be a fun story of a weird tattoo shop in Cancun, that was for sure. It was a stupid idea, but it was too late to stop it.

"My buddy Thomas, who I was living with, and selling with, decided one day he wanted to be a tattoo artist—an apprentice, is what they called him. I was on some…well, something, anyway. I was high, and he convinced me to let him tattoo a string of music notes on my thigh, like a high school theater kid. It came out okay, though. And he just kept going, on me, on the guys, especially on himself—he was even more covered than I am, even back then. Shit, probably even more by now.

"At first, I really liked 'em. My face ones, when I got them. They were my idea. I liked feeling like I had a mask on, because no one ever saw my young face that couldn't grow a beard—still can't, actually. They just saw this badass gangster with all these tattoos. And I *wanted* to look badass, not like I was still a kid, even though I was. So that was cool. And through Thomas they were free, so I just kept getting more."

So, I know he said "gangster," but in context, I don't think it actually proved anything. Definitely perked my ears, though.

"But…so one day," he went on. "I saw my grandmother, from across the street. Caught her eye. We were both trying to cross this intersection at the same time. First time I'd seen her in over two years, and I was thinking, 'What in the world does she need over this way?' There was nothing around but a bunch of residentials. Anyway, I smiled a little, and she looked away, not a hint of recognition. Just a little fear, actually. And then she looked down at her watch—the fakest thing—and did this." He slapped his palm against his forehead, his mouth in a little O. "And scuttled back the other way. I could totally tell she was acting. At first, I thought she might have been angry and didn't want to talk to me, like she was avoiding me, but when we crossed, I saw my reflection in a car window and I realized, nah, she was afraid of this gangster badass with all the tattoos on his face. I looked like a gangster, but I didn't look at all like myself. So much so that my own grandmother didn't recognize me.

"So that began my desire to take off all my masks. The tattoos, the drugs. I wanted to erase that part of me completely—body and skin. A blank slate. First part's done, the drugs. The lifestyle's done. The tattoos, turns out, will be harder. Well, maybe not harder, but definitely more expensive."

He smiled at the desk, not looking up at me. I nodded, kind of passive. The mask metaphor stuck with me.

"When did you get into the, even-out-your-karma thing?"

He deflated a little. "That wasn't until recently. But I dunno. You said something a while back, asking if doing something just for the good karma means I'm being selfish, and kind of cancels out the good karma to begin with. Kind of fucked with me, to be honest."

I felt a hot blush creep up my neck. "Oh, I'm sorry, I—I didn't mean to make—"

"No, I'm glad you did. It made me think a lot about selfishness and good intentions, and…I think what we're doing here is good. I like talking to you, and I like helping you. And you're also helping me, and maybe you're also feeling good about helping me. Even we're only helping to feel good, even if it's selfish, we're still…" He dragged his thumb down the side of his face, massaging into his jaw muscle. "I dunno. Maybe not."

"I mean, I don't know what I'm talking about. You know?" I squirmed a little. I never expect to be impactful to other people's lives. "You're not so scary to me, by the way," I added after a pause. "But I guess I can see how a little old lady might get freaked out."

I kind of said it like a joke to lighten the mood, but I'm not sure if it came off that way. I don't think he really felt like having a lighter mood, anyway. I took a breath and tried again.

"I liked what you said about masks. I think I 'took off a mask' when my mom died."

Billy met my eye with slightly pursed lips, listening. I realized he might not know she's dead. I couldn't remember if I'd told him or not.

"All my old friends in Somerville," I began again. "I told them all point blank that she died of a drug overdose. I just didn't care if they knew or not anymore. I'd gone to such lengths to hide her addiction when she was alive—never brought anyone over, never introduced her to anyone else's parents, whatever. But I was so emotionally numb when she died, nothing else seemed to matter anymore. They were all really cool about it, even as twelve-year-olds. It felt nice to tell them the truth. So, I guess I learned taking off your mask usually feels better than suffocating with it on."

Billy jabbed his finger into the bunny head resting on the desk. "Yeah, you got that right." He looked like he was going to ask a question, but thought better of it, so I was left to think over that lesson in silence.

You know what sucks? I *knew* that lesson, from then. I already *knew* it's easier and better in the long run to be yourself, but I was still, even then—literally, *that day*—hiding my gayness from my dad. And I *knew* I should focus on the good and not the bad, but my brain wouldn't listen.

I know the lessons, so why can't I put them in practice? It's frustrating. I feel like such an idiot sometimes.

Billy leaned back in his chair, closing his fists over his eyes, forehead. "I can't wait—" he flung his fingers, like he was shaking off mud,"—to get this shit off of me." He laughed a little. "God. These tattoos! God..."

I checked my watch. "Well, for the moment, you'll have to settle for just covering them back up again."

He took the head in his hands, smoothed his fingers over the fur on the cheeks, then eased it on and became the bunny again.

Eighteen

The Man of the Hour

Okay. So, this is part of the story nobody really knows. The cops and the journalists didn't ask me any questions about anything that happened before—not because I'm a minor, since I'm not. I think they just wanted to hear from Max, since he's the boss. But even if they did ask me questions, I don't think I would've remembered this moment happening at the time, with so much else going on.

I was on cash, a day or so after Billy and I were talking about masks. Max was on camera. Kathi had the day off. It was slow, maybe around two in the afternoon, when a group of guys in sweatshirts caught my eye. The register faces a balcony sidelined by escalators, though the "up" escalator wasn't working this week. I liked watching who hesitated, wondering if they were allowed to climb up an unmoving escalator. Sometimes people walked down it, which confused me. The sweatshirt guys did just that—climbing down the up escalator, joking and pointing at the other set of stairs, apparently realizing their mistake.

One of them laughed—and I felt my blood run cold. A big black bird on his chin. It was the same guy as before, the one who had had the lollipop.

They came right up to my desk. I did my best to act normal.

"Hello," I said flatly as they approached.

The lollipop guy leaned both his elbows on my desk. I could smell him—body spray and dandruff. Another started shaking the sample-photo snowglobe.

"Hey," the lollipop guy said. "Is this shit only for kids, or what?"

I stammered a little. We got a lot of goofy teens—even, to my eternal embarrassment, some kids from my high school—but no adults who ever wanted their picture with the bunny like this. Certainly, no thirty-ish-year-olds like these guys.

Then Max appeared at my elbow. "Everyone can see the bunny! Young and old."

The guys bounded past me to Billy, who waved stiffly with one paw. Max said something quick and low about how I should never turn away a customer, no matter how weird, and I nodded, watching over his shoulder. One of the guys jumped on Billy's lap, another perched on the chair beside him. Lollipop Guy stood and flicked the bunny's ears.

"Eh, what's up, doc?" Lollipop Guy said out the corner of his mouth. "Got a sweet gig here, eh, doc?"

"He's a dick, not a doc," another said, and they snickered.

Something deep in my stomach told me to run, but my legs were frozen. I felt unsafe turning my back on them, but even less safe facing them. I turned and pretended to mess with the register. I checked the paper on the receipt printer thingy. Half empty.

Flash. Finally. Their photo popped up on the second screen. One guy, the one on Billy's chair, was doing the dumb circle game thing with his finger and thumb by his side. The one on his lap had his back pin-straight and hands folded on his knee, like a doll. The one standing was the only one whose menacing smile matched his appearance.

I had to force myself to ask if they wanted to purchase a photo. They bought the cheapest package.

"Who knows if we'll ever all be in the same picture again, right?" Lollipop Guy said. Another smiled into his crossed arms. "Thanks for letting us meet the man of the hour."

And then they left.

No one else was in line, so once the guys were out of sight, Max waved me over to huddle around Billy.

"So, do we know those guys?"

"Those guys?" Billy asked from behind the mask. It was super weird to hear the bunny talk with Billy's voice, especially out here on set.

Max tilted his chin and raised his brows. "Yeah, the guys that just came through?"

"My dad was talking to them the other day," I said. "He said they've been hanging around here."

Max flicked his eyes from me back to Billy.

Billy didn't move a muscle. "They're some old buddies. They think it's funny I'm the Easter Bunny."

Max nodded, planting his hands on his hips. "Well,

they have their picture, so hopefully they won't come back again? We don't want to scare off the soccer moms."

"Got it," Billy said.

Then some little girls got in line, and we took their picture. And I tried to calm my jittery hands, but it was like, four cups of coffee. I'm jittering a little now, just thinking about it.

Nineteen

Unpacking

The next day, when we had a break together, I asked Billy who the guys were, point blank.

"I told you and Max, didn't I? They were some old buddies. I knew them in the city."

"Were they the guys you lived with?"

He took a deep pull on his cigarette. It took me like thirty seconds to realize he didn't intend to answer.

"Okay…well, why are they here?"

"I don't know. But don't worry about them."

"They were here before, too. Don't—"

"Just chill."

I lifted my bag of trail mix and dropped it on my lap in exasperation. They shook around a bit, and one little peanut jumped out and onto the floor. "How on earth do you expect me to chill? Who are they? What are they doing here? How do they know you? What's with the lollipop?"

"Maybe he's trying to quit smoking. Not like it'll work."

"Oh my god, I don't care about the lollipop—*who are they?* You want good karma so bad? Tell me who those scary dudes are before they rob us at gunpoint!"

It was kind of a dick move to bring up the karma thing,

since I knew he was working through that, but I was getting desperate.

Billy rolled his head back on his neck. "Dude, whatever. You want a story?" He met my eyes, then quickly darted them away. "I sold those guys out, five years ago, and they all went to jail. Way more than just them—like, eight guys. Okay? One of my clients…well, I just couldn't sell anymore, but it doesn't—they're just fucking with me."

"Mad at you?"

"Probably. I don't think many of them were in prison for long, but it was definitely a big deal."

"Are you in danger?"

"No."

I raised my eyebrows.

"Not every dealer—" he gritted his teeth. "No. Look, they sold drugs, but I don't think they're gonna hurt me. They're not killers, not on purpose. I'm just gonna have to see them soon, probably. They'll yell and I'll take it and they'll never want to see me again. Maybe they'll beat me up, probably not. It's not like I didn't know this was coming. I'm just kind of surprised those dumbasses actually managed to track me down."

He gave me these wide, pleading eyes. Before that moment, I thought he was annoyed at me, but now I realized there was a lot more going on than that.

"And the lesson? I learned I can betray people," he said. "And be real selfish, and sell out my friends and get off scot-free. I learned I'm great at running away. And I learned I can rack up some real bad karma. And that's not even…" he looked away, hid his mouth behind his fist. "Can you tell me a completely unrelated story, please?"

"Um, yeah," I said, softly. "Okay."

There was so much to—like you say—unpack there, but he needed a distraction more than I needed to dig into his personal life. I told my brain to trust him that the guys weren't dangerous, but another part of my brain insisted that they were. And even though that second part was being "negative," I wasn't sure if it wasn't also correct.

I tried to put it all aside and think about the furthest possible thing from jail and drugs and karma and negativity.

And I saw Nora in my mind.

I was kind of surprised at my own brain. Nora was the *pinnacle* of negativity at the moment. We were still not speaking to one another. But I didn't see her in the treehouse, I saw her onstage, with her black electric bass and her shaggy hair and her arms full of tight bracelets and hair elastics she never uses.

"My friend Nora plays an incredible bass in a jazz band," I said. "Whenever I watch her…I mean, she's always really pretty. But when she's playing, she's just…"

I mean, how was I supposed to describe something that takes my breath away?

"She gets this look in her eye like she's vibing, driving in the sunset, her head bobbing, eyes closed—you know? And she always performs in black and white striped shirts and these big, strappy black boots, shiny leather, they go up to her knees. She's *so* cool. Watching her, I'm like, jealous and turned on all at the same time."

I said the last part as a joke, mostly, to make him smile,

and it worked. But it was also sort of true, I think. True enough to distract me off the gangsters for the time being.

"One time she devoted a song to me, at a concert: 'To my friend, who's more than just a friend, Mo.' And I thought she meant it one way, and she meant it another. This was all after this other time when a similar mis-understanding happened. Anyway, that was an awkward couple days, and I guess I learned...to always ask questions. Even if the answer isn't what you want to hear. Because it's better than just being left in the dark and guessing. It's better to know the truth, even if it hurts."

I didn't exactly mean that to be a pointed statement, but it probably felt that way to Billy.

Twenty

So that weekend, Elise invited me over to her apartment for the first time. It was probably the best night of my life, so sorry if this is...I don't know. I just want to remember everything. And I want to tell you everything.

Elise had this idea on our first date that she'd cook me my first true-blue vegetarian dinner. I was pretty sure I'd had plenty of meatless dinners in my life, but I agreed anyway. I'd agree to almost anything that meant spending more time with Elise. I said that since it was my "first" vegetarian dinner, she'll have to do a "first," too, and watch *The Shining* with me afterward. It didn't take much convincing.

I know it's cliché, but I tried on, like, eight different outfits before deciding on *just* the right purple-and-black flannel.

I was really excited.

Elise asked if I'd mind swinging by the grocery store on the way and grabbing some vegetables. She sent me a list. I wandered around the produce section, looking at the prices carefully. Nothing she wanted was too expensive, but the issue with working at twelve dollars an hour was that a meal's worth of vegetables was suddenly an hour's pay. And

I had a feeling Elise wouldn't want to settle for non-organic. Well, she probably would, but I didn't want to disappoint her.

It was kind of dumb to get hung up on the price of a few veggies, since I hardly spent any money on anything except weed. Not like I had any bills to pay. But it seemed even dumber to spend an hour's pay when I could just slip half the stuff into my backpack, so I did that instead. I bought the egg noodles to avoid suspicion, and threw out the receipt on the way out of the store. I felt so smart when I threw out that receipt. Shoplifting? Not a problem. Elise finding out I shoplifted? End of the world. But I threw out the receipt, so now Elise would never know I stole something!

Yeah. That lasted.

Anyway, Elise lived in Lowell, which was a farther drive away from the mall than I expected, in a junky multifamily covered with peeling white paint. A little wooden blue jay hung on a nail in the front door, swinging in the wind, her address on its wing. I thought I would have to pay for parking, but the morning of, while discussing which vegetables I should buy, she texted me that I could park on the street next to the liquor store for free. It was kind of sketchy, but I figured she'd know what was okay and what wasn't.

Elise was on the second floor, she said, but I had no idea how to get in, so I just stood slightly off the sidewalk and called her. I kicked at an empty nip bottle while her phone rang.

"Hey! You outside?" A couch or bed groaned in the background—she must have sat up as she answered.

"Hi! Yes."

"Be right down."

She hung up, and in just under ten seconds she appeared out of a side door near the back of the house. I never would have thought to try that door. You could hardly even see it from the road.

Elise was looking adorable as always. Her hair was tied up in two buns, one on either side of her head, and a bright blue headband tied at the nape of her neck, ribboning down across her shoulder. She was wearing pink slippers. She kissed me, and I smelled garlic and ginger.

"Sorry, this place is so hard to find, I know," she said, and I stuttered back something like, "Oh yeah, cool, no worries," and followed her up the creaking wooden stairs. On the off-white plaster wall of the staircase—the whole place dimly lit—hung various movie posters and a few crumpled up children's drawings on white lined paper. At the top of the stairs was a tiny landing where I toed off my canvas shoes, then Elise pushed aside a bunch of those multicolor, doorway bead things so I could follow her into her apartment.

I'd never been in a college apartment before. The room was cozy, with white curtains cutting the sunlight and fairy lights strung around the ceiling. A big green sofa and a couple bean bag chairs faced a TV, which hung over what looked like a fake fireplace. On the coffee table a bong, an ashtray, and a stack of textbooks fought for space with a stack of crusty dishes and mugs filled with dregs of coffee or dried-up tea bags. On the walls, more movie posters.

"Sorry, it's a mess in here. It's always a mess in here." Elise led me through the living room to the connected kitchen, separated only by a peeling Formica breakfast bar. I took a seat at one of the teal-cushioned stools, resting my backpack on the floor and hiking the plastic bag of groceries (including the ones who made their way out of the store in my backpack) onto the counter.

"Got all you needed! I think. I couldn't find Vidalia onions so I just got a normal one."

"That's fine!" She peered into the bag and took out the onion, the portobello mushrooms, the egg noodles, the sour cream. "You ever have a *prima, delicioso,* pure-vegetarian mushroom stroganoff?"

I've never even had a beef stroganoff. Actually, I only knew the phrase because I'd heard it once on TV, on a cooking show. My mom used to love watching those when she was conked out. She watched a lot of different shows, but she only watched dumb ones when she was really high, so she wouldn't miss anything important. I shook my head, a bit nervous that I wouldn't like it, but I liked all the ingredients, so how bad could it be?

"Can I help you with anything?"

"Nope! It's super easy. Just get ready to be converted." She winked, bent down to grab a pot out of the cupboard and filled it with water from the sink. She had on heathered sweatpants that pooled around her slippers. They looked cozy. I wanted to run my hands over them.

I had to find something to talk about. We'd so rarely

been in a situation like this, where there was nothing to distract us from each other. The kitchen/living room was pretty simple. I scoured it for a conversation topic and settled on the poster.

"Lots of movie posters," I said, dumbly. "I've never seen that one."

I gestured to the first one to my right. The poster was mostly comprised of an Asian man's face, looking like he was in pain as he drove a car into the night. In the upper-right corner must have been the title and other info, but it was all written in (I think) Korean. Elise, setting down a cutting board, glanced up to see which one I meant.

"Oh, yeah. Me neither. It's called *As I Lay Dreaming* or, *As I Lay Dying*, something like that. My roommate, Kira, is a film student. She goes to all these premieres and festivals and gets all these posters at them. For free, I think."

"Oh! That's cool. I love movies."

"I know, yeah! I thought of her when we were talking about *Rear Window*. She won't be around until later, but I'm sure you'll like her if you get to meet her."

"Maybe she'll watch *The Shining* with us after dinner," I said, though I kind of wanted Elise to myself.

"Yeah, maybe," Elise said, and I was happy to hear a touch of reluctance in her voice. "She could definitely tell you more about *all* the posters. And she will, whether you ask her or not."

I nodded, suddenly realizing something. "Are any of your other roommates home?"

"No, not right now. Kira's on a set for a project and Ann and Mills are out somewhere." She paused, glancing up at the cabinets in thought for a moment. "Actually, I think Mills went home for the weekend. Whatever. But nah, we're home alone."

Home alone. The words echoed around in my head. I wondered which of the doors down the short hallway belonged to her bedroom, and I wondered if that was where she intended things to go after dinner, before *The Shining*. Or even instead of *The Shining*. It made me wish dinner was over already.

"How are your classes?" I asked, because I needed to say something.

"Fine. Ooh, I finally got into some real psych classes this semester. Finally. Of course, turns out I don't actually like them."

Yeah, so I didn't actually know what her "major" was until that moment. My other high school friends and I were so tired about talking about colleges and futures I never asked about that sort of stuff anymore, but obviously in college you must like talking about it. Considering it is then your life. So, she wanted to be a psychologist—or, used to.

"Why not?"

"A lot of worst-case scenarios, and a *lot* of memorization." She was chopping up the onion now, and the loud knife punctuated her frustration. "I have such a shit memory and…I dunno. Just not what I thought it was, and now I'm already jaded. I just don't know what to switch to, if I'm going to switch. I don't know. *And* I'm already two years in at this school, so I don't want to switch *schools*, you know? But I only went here for the psych program and…God. I don't know. Maybe I should just stick it out and see if they get better. It's hard to know the right thing to do."

"Jeez. I thought identity crises were supposed to happen *before* you chose a college."

She laughed, high and lofty. "Ugh, you have no idea."

Then it was quiet again. I have no idea why it was suddenly awkward to be around her. Maybe because she was cooking and I had nothing to do? Or maybe because I knew nothing about college? Or maybe because there was this tension in the air because we were home alone together for the first time.

It *couldn't* be awkward with her. This *had* to go well. Luckily, thanks to Billy, I knew a great way to fill a silence

"Um. Do you want to play a game? While you cook?"

"Sure. What kind of game? I mean, it'll have to be a pretty hands-free game."

She waved around the big kitchen knife, the kind I'm too scared to use at home, as a joke. Then she used it to scoop up the diced onion and toss it in a frying pan. When she did that, she put the blade against the heel of her palm, and I almost shouted out to her to be careful. She obviously knew what she was doing, but I had no idea how to deal with an injury like that, if it happened. I had no idea how to cook, and I had no idea about college. I had no idea how to deal with being alone with Elise, and I had no idea how to deal with *Elise*, really. I just suddenly felt *so* in over my head.

The stove was on the other side of the kitchen, so her back was to me as she dumped the onion in. Not having to look at her eyes for a minute let me catch my breath, take a break from smiling. Okay. I had to calm down.

"It's a story game," I said, after a pause that was just a little too long. The onion started sizzling immediately. She also scooped in a small cup of garlic and ginger, which I guessed she'd cut up ahead of time.

"Okay. How do you play?"

"Um…" *Play* wasn't really an appropriate word for it, and my so-called "game" suddenly seemed super lame. Only *I* could invent a game with an ex-gangster covered in face tattoos and have it turn out totally lame. Telling stories? Deciphering the morals? I tried to think of a quick alternative on the fly, but I couldn't think of any other story game, so I just explained it. "Basically, you just tell a story from your life, and what you learned from it—"

"Oh, gotcha! And then the other person has to tell a story from their life with the same lesson?"

I can't even explain the relief that flooded through me. It was a little different from what I did with Billy, but she'd actually made it a *game*. "Yes!"

"And is this the one where—are there questions involved?"

I wasn't sure how there could be. "No, I think that's a different one."

"Okay! I played something like this at camp, once. Do you want to go first, or should I?"

"You can go first." My voice was getting weaker by the minute.

"Okay, cool. Great. Just let me think of a good one." She dumped the pasta in the boiling water and started washing off the mushrooms in the sink, humming theatrically. Suddenly she looked up at me, her eyes wide, long eyelashes flared up and nearly hitting her brows. "Oh! Are you thirsty? I have some sodas. Or do you want a real drink?"

She opened the fridge, started to list off various drinks of the alcoholic and non-alcoholic varieties. I had to drive home later, and through the city to boot, but I thought one drink this early in the night wouldn't do any harm. Especially if my goal was to be less awkward.

"Is it...too early for a 'real' drink?"

"Not on my calendar," she said, and went right for the bottles of cider. She opened them with something off her set of keys. I had never had the brand before, and it was so bubbly it burned my nose, but it was much better than the strong beers John liked so much. I sipped aggressively while she began her story, desperate to hit a level of buzz that would let my muscles relax a little.

"Okay, okay, here's a story. My parents took my sister and me to France our freshman year of high school. It was amazing—they let us drink wine, which was super wild, and we went into these crazy catacombs with all these skeletons—like, *real* skeletons and skulls and stuff in the walls. Dude. It was unreal."

I put on a goofy face, a sarcastic voice. "I thought you said they were *real*, not *unreal*."

She rolled her eyes. "It was *unreal* how *real* they were. Anyway, we saw the Eiffel Tower, obviously. And it was... both bigger and smaller than you'd imagine. Like, in movies it kind of towers over everything, and it doesn't really do that in real life. My mom told me not to get too excited, so I figured it would just be this little, *thing*. Like a statue, or a fountain-sized thing. But it wasn't, it was actually kind of big. Taller than the mall, probably. And there's stairs, you can climb up it. We didn't, but, you could. So, we got all the stereotypical photos of the Eiffel Tower from you know, two hundred feet away or whatever. And then we walked underneath it, and we all got a picture of us looking down at the camera, like…" She held her phone down by her thigh and leaned over it, the ribbons of her headband swaying off her shoulder. "…in a huddle. And this super-hot dude walks by us and says, in this super thick French accent, 'Ah, yes, the finest upskirt shot of *La Tour Eiffel.*'"

She laughed, and I laughed too—mostly at her horrendous impersonation of a French accent. "So, what did you learn from that?"

"Oh, easy. Super-hot French dude, super-hot upskirt. It was my bisexual awakening."

"Oh, obviously. How didn't I catch that?"

"I have no idea. Thought you were smarter than that."

"Boy, did I have you fooled."

Another smile. It gave me almost as much confidence as the third-of-a-bottle I'd already downed.

"Okay, your turn. Different story, same message. Go."

"Well, that will be difficult. I don't have a bisexual awakening story, but I might have a lesbian awakening story. Does that count?"

She sighed dramatically. "I mean…I *suppose*. Kind of breaking the rules, but. I guess."

"Thank you for your flexibility."

She snickered into the sizzling onions a bit longer than our sarcasm deserved, and though I wasn't sure exactly what was on her mind I could guess it was an innuendo on "her flexibility," and since I knew I wouldn't be able to react suavely to it I just sped on with my story.

"So, I was in eighth grade, and there was this girl—" Nora. "—who was the first of our group to get a boyfriend. A *real* boyfriend, not just the middle school, sit-next-to-me-on-the-bus kind of boyfriend. And I was beyond jealous. She was dating Stevie Fitch, like, the most sought-after boy in school. I didn't really see it—"

"Wonder why."

"Right? But I knew he was attractive. I'm not *blind*. I'm just not straight."

"And she is."

"As a board." I took another sip. "Is that the phrase?"

"I don't think so."

"Whatever. She was straight. Still is."

"All the hot ones are." Elise looked over her shoulder and added, "Except you, luckily."

"She added as an afterthought."

"No!"

"No!" I imitated. She acted like she was going to throw her tongs at me so convincingly I actually flinched. "Hey! Violence is not necessary."

"Your sass is not necessary."

"Your...*ass* is not necessary."

"Oh—wanna bet?"

She shook her hips a little at me, looking over her

shoulder with a feisty smile. I shook my head, grinning at the ceiling. *Wow* she was cute.

"You're distracting me from my story."

"Okay, okay, I'll stop."

"So—" she gave another little shake without looking away from the pan, and I giggled. *"Anyway,* it's pretty typical. I saw them kiss one day outside, as we were all going out to the busses. And like, the biggest cliché, I was super jealous, but I realized while fuming on the bus that I didn't want to kiss frickin' Stevie at all. I wanted to kiss *her.* He had done this thing where he put his hand on her cheek, and her ear was between his first and second finger, you know? And I just wanted to do that, to have just my fingertips in her hair while we kissed. And it was a lot to take in all at once. I mean, it's not like it was the nineties or something. I knew being gay existed, and I was cool with it. I just didn't realize it applied to *me* until that moment. And I still didn't fully realize or accept it yet, but over the next couple years I came into my own."

"So…when did you finally get to do that?"

"Do what?"

"Not with her, obviously. But…when was your first kiss?"

Oh, jeez. "…isn't it your turn to tell a story?"

Elise tilted her head. "Well, fair. I can tell you my first kiss if you want, first."

"Okay."

"I was thirteen and Robbie Waters kissed me at the end of a school dance, before immediately running off into the crowd so our parents wouldn't see us together."

"Romantic."

"Yeah, I sold the rights to John Hughes last year."

I didn't get it, but I laughed anyway. Later I looked it up, and felt like the worst movie fan in the world for not remembering he was the *Breakfast Club* guy.

"Okay, your turn."

"Mine was with this girl—" Nora. "—who was…oh, what do you call it?" I could hear it in her voice, too. Then it came to me. "*Experimenting.*"

Elise glanced back, a pained look on her face. "Ouch."

"Yeah."

"I mean, I get it, I respect exploring your sexuality but…when people play with other people's emotions…"

She tried a weak smile. I returned it.

"Yeah. That's pretty much what happened. She thought she was gay for a week so we kissed. Like, a lot." And I got to ease my hands into her hair, her ear between my first and second finger. "And we held hands at the movies once, for a whole movie. I was half in love with her when she told me she made a mistake and she actually thought she was straight. We were freshmen. And we're still friends, kind of, or well, like—"

"Wait," Elise said, turning around, ignoring the food. "Is *that* the girl whose house we egged?"

"Um…" Shit. She's so smart. "Yeah, actually."

"Ohhh," she said. "I get it now."

And you know the weird thing? *I* didn't get it until she said that. And it hit me like a ton of bricks.

Was I actually only mad at Nora because of what she'd done to me three years ago?

Three years ago. It was something we hadn't talked about since. I remember biking home from her house in tears, hands shaking so bad on the handlebars I swerved and got honked at by a pick-up.

Elise turned off the burners. "Shit, dude. I'm sorry." She met my eye while she poured the pasta into a colander, already in the sink. "If it makes you feel better, I'm a card-carrying bisexual. Proven and tested."

"Oh, really?"

She fought a smile, grabbed her wallet off the seat beside me, and handed me a rainbow business card that read: Elise Hale: Official Bisexual.

I couldn't help laughing. I actually laughed so hard it would have been embarrassing, if it hadn't been with Elise, and she wasn't laughing, too. Once I caught my breath, I held up the card and said, "Do you just carry this around for that one joke? How long have you kept this in your wallet?"

"Yes, and…" She started laughing again. "Maybe four years?"

I hadn't laughed that hard in forever.

The food was ready before long. We ate on the couch, our drinks on the crowded coffee table. I worked hard not to spill anything (although I doubt you would have been able to tell if I did) and tried to eat as much as possible. I used to be able to eat so much more than I do now, but I finished about three quarters of the plate, which is a lot for me nowadays.

The cider really hit about halfway through dinner. I drink even less than I eat, so I was probably tipsier than I should have been with that much alcohol. And she was so pretty, and I was getting so nervous.

Full disclosure, kissing Nora those few times was my only "experience" before Elise. So, I was sure I was bad, and even if I wasn't bad, I had no idea how to do anything beyond kissing. But something about Elise—nervous as I was—made me comfortable. Like she wouldn't mind if I needed some teaching, some help. Like she'd just enjoy spending time with me, even if I wasn't any good yet. She seemed to enjoy spending time with me despite my horribly lame flirting, so maybe...

"Not so bad for a meatless dinner, huh?"

"It's delicious," I said, and it was.

And then I put my plate on the table next to hers, on top of a philosophy textbook, and with the plates out of the way she scooted closer to me, and then her knee was touching mine. I had on jeans with the knees cut out, so I could feel those soft sweatpants on my skin, and her knee underneath them. She took my hand and started kind of running her thumb along the inside of my palm.

"So," she said in a soft, lower voice. "We could keep playing that game...or we could watch an old movie, like the ones you like..."

My gaze was locked on her knee, but now I looked up at her a little with just my eyes. She was really close to me, smiling with a little bit of mischief on her lips.

"Or we could...do whatever else you wanted to do," she said, smiling. "Ladies' choice."

"Well, what's *your* choice, lady?"

"Mm…want to see my game collection? Maybe we can play something together?"

What a line. I said yes, and she led me by the hand down the hallway and into one of the bedrooms. Blue floor lights lined the perimeter of the unmade bed, looking like something off a spaceship. Plastic shelves held food, books, and a metallic Eiffel Tower, and her clothes hung in a tiny closet, mismatched and half falling off their hangers. Elise scoffed when she saw the closet.

"My roommate's stupid cat. She always tries to climb up my clothes."

She rehung a few shirts, then gestured to the bed. "Under there are all the games, if you want to take a look at them."

I had had a strong feeling that the "game collection" was just a ploy to get me into the bedroom—and a poorly disguised one at that—but the amount of board games had me reconsidering her ulterior motives. I didn't know the names of any of these games—but then I saw a slick black box behind them. A leather handle was on the top. I pulled it out and undid a couple metal latches to reveal a ukulele.

"You play ukulele?"

Elise snorted, left the rest of the clothes as they were and knelt beside me on the floor. "Oh, my god. There was like, this whole *phase* in high school where everyone wanted to play a quirky instrument. This one was cheap. And it's pronounced *ooh-koo-laylay*, you uncultured swine."

"Really?"

"Yeah. If you don't believe me, ask everyone I pretentiously corrected back in the day."

I pulled it out by its neck, gently. Carved on the body was a little lizard and a swirly sun. I ran my thumb over the strings, and they sang out a grisly out-of-tune chord. We both grimaced a little.

"Oh, jeez." Elise took it from me, kneeling beside me, and tuned it gently by ear. Then she strummed a simple chord to test it. It still wasn't quite right, but good enough. She played a few chords, this way and that, swaying side to side on her knees.

It's never not hot when someone you like plays music for you. Even if it's kinda out of tune. I leaned against her bed, swooning, watching her eyes watch the strings, then watching her bandaged fingers shift from one chord to the next.

After a moment, coming out of a romantic stupor, I reached out and placed my hand over her left hand, running my thumb over her fingers, still pressing into the strings. Her strumming slowed to a stop.

"What's up with these bandages?" I asked, something I'd wanted to know since I met her. "You always seem to have them."

She smiled sadly down at her hands, then twisted her right hand so I could see the outer corner of her thumb— one of only four fingers without a bandage. It was red raw, the cuticle and the skin around her nail flaring in hangnails and tiny lacerations.

"I bite my nails a little," she said, which wasn't even accurate, never mind the fact that it was the understatement of the year. Her nails were fine—short, but not bitten short.

"Well, I bite my fingers, I guess," she corrected, as if she could read my mind.

"Why?"

The question left my lips before I could edit it. I half expected her to wince, but she just shrugged.

"Anxiety." She shrank her hand away, but I held onto it. "Um...it's so gross, I know, but I...have been trying to stop..."

I didn't know what I was doing. I didn't know if she'd find it weird or what, but since I didn't know what to say, I didn't say anything and just took her hands in mine. The uke fell onto her lap. I walked a couple inches closer on my knees, then kissed each of her fingers, one by one, lifting her hands to my lips. After the last one, I looked up and saw the strangest, most mysterious expression—I could hardly explain it. Somewhere between bewilderment and gratefulness. It was only there for a second before she threw her kissed fingertips into my hair and kissed me, pushing me up against the side of her bed.

I probably shouldn't go into all this with you. I don't know. Whatever. You can skip ahead if you want.

But the main thing is, after a *while* kissing on the floor, I pulled away and said, "What if we—" she kissed me again. I laughed and pulled away again. "What if we got *on* the bed?"

And she pulled back to look me in the eye, her eyebrows knitting together in concern just a little. "Yeah?"

"Yeah."

She smiled slowly. "You sure?"

"I'm sure it's super uncomfortable on the floor, yeah," I joked, and she rolled her eyes playfully.

I kissed that mole on her neck, *finally,* after so many moments longing to, but then she pushed away gently to look me seriously in the eye.

"I mean…are you sure you want to…? Because we don't have to."

There wasn't too much time between when she asked and when I answered, but I did think about it. I thought about how much I liked her, and how much I wanted to have sex with her, and how safe and loved and *understood* I felt when I was with her, more than I ever had with anybody before. And I really hoped I made her feel the same way.

I just want you to know that when I told her yes, I meant it. And she meant it when she agreed. And my *god* it was wonderful.

Twenty-One

My Rights

The next day I was in a daze of happiness for the whole day at school, and it didn't even falter until work when I overheard a crazy mother go nuts at Max about prices. This wasn't anything new. It happened several times a week and, to be fair, our cheapest package was thirty-five dollars and it was wallet-sized photos only.

This woman was ape-shit mad, clutching a fussy toddler to her chest and screaming in his ear while Max tried to calm her down, his hands held gently open up in front of him like she was a spooked horse or something. Or an alpaca, since I guess that's what he's used to.

I was glad I wasn't on cash this time. Usually when I start getting yelled at for not giving them free photos and they ask for a manager, Max takes the brunt of it anyway (and it seems to roll right off of him), but it's never fun for me to get yelled at. Even if, afterward, Max pats me on the shoulder and shit-talks the angry customer before telling me what I already knew: that I hadn't done anything wrong.

You can meet the bunny for free, but the cheapest photo-set is thirty-five dollars. It's just how it is.

"I'm very sorry. I hope you enjoy your photos," Max said as the woman gave a condescending pout of a smile.

She thanked him for the free 5x7 he threw in to make her shut up and walked off. Then Max turned his back to the line of customers, looked right at me, and mouthed, "What a bitch."

I usually fumed over the complaining customers, angry that their lives were apparently so perfect they had only this to complain about. Today, I wondered if I was any better.

After all—I may not have the money Max does or the alive, married parents Nora does, but I do have a dad who was cool enough to put me in therapy without thinking it made him a bad parent, or telling me it was all in my head, or refusing for his own pride. He took my five-out-of-seven symptoms of depression seriously and did what he thought would help. We weren't starving. I didn't *have* to work, to pay the rent, or anything. He pays for my phone bill and car insurance, unlike Claire's parents—but not gas, like John's do.

And I had a wonderful girlfriend. How could my life be bad when Elise was in it?

How could it be good when my mom is—*ugh.*

God. It was giving me a headache. Did I have it bad or not? Did I have a right to complain, like Claire said, or was I being over-dramatic? I know you said everyone needs help sometimes, but...was that true? Really?

I had to find out.

I'd never actually told anyone the full story of my mom's death before, and maybe it was a strange choice, but I figured there were only so many workdays left until Easter, and after that I may never see Billy again. So, I decided, as I walked him to our break...fuck it.

"Ready for another story?" Billy asked, pulling out a sandwich.

"Yeah," I said. "Actually, I wanna skip to the big ones."

"Oh, yeah?"

"Can't take the suspense," I said, with the approximation of a smile.

"Okay." He crossed his arms, leaned back. "Should I go first this time?"

"Actually, can I?"

"By all means."

So, I took a breath and I told him:

"My mom's dead. She was an opioid addict. Got on them after a simple surgery. Never got off."

I paused. That was usually where I stopped. People didn't ask questions past that point. But this time, I made myself keep going.

"Eventually, her prescription ran out so she called her old weed dealers from college, and when they didn't know anyone, she tried her dealer from high school. One of them knew a guy who knew a guy who sold the pills she was on. But they weren't cheap.

"I was young when it started, and she told me all the money was going to her 'doctor,' who she called Ronald. I remember the name because—"

"Ronald McDonald?" He smiled wryly, eyes not leaving his sandwich.

I smiled. "Like I said, I was a little kid. So, I pictured a doctor with clown makeup the whole time. Demanding money. Kinda morbid.

"Anyway, Mom burned through her paycheck, then

dipped into retirement savings, the savings they had for a house, the whole shebang. Still mostly the painkillers, but some other stuff too, and her bills racked up. Started pawning her jewelry, until Dad caught on and hid some of her nicer stuff, and her stuff that used to be his mother's, in the gun safe. I learned all this afterward, but, yeah. All her money, right to Ronald.

"So then came the shoplifting." I shifted in my seat, not looking him in the eye anymore. "She taught me how to do it, when I got older. How to only hit the places that wouldn't notice, or at least wouldn't mind a missing piece or two. Never hit a locally owned place. She was still a suburban lady at heart. Loved supporting local businesses."

I paused. This was always where the story got fuzzy. Billy stared in rapt attention, the sandwich hovering between the desk and his mouth.

"So, I don't know what happened, exactly. Dad said after she caught herself taking money out of my college fund, she tried to quit and then, a few weeks later, overdosed on a relapse, when she tried to take her original dosage again but her tolerance was down. I don't know if that's true. I kind of think he's just trying to make both of us feel better— like, with a fantasy that she tried to quit for me but her sickness got the better of her."

"That could be true," Billy offered, his voice low and serious, his body still.

"Maybe. Maybe it was just a dumb mistake, but I don't know. Maybe she was trying to quit. Maybe Ronald fucked her over and sold her laced pills or something. Personally, I kind of think it was suicide." I rubbed my nose, held back the tears I could feel forming. "Maybe seeing her preteen daughter steal bras so she could pay for drugs made her suicidal. But whatever. It doesn't actually matter what happened; the important thing is that neither of us stopped her when we could have. And she died, in June, almost five years ago. Dad found her on the couch when he came home for lunch. I was in school. I didn't get to see her until she was already dead in the hospital bed."

They had dressed her in a light blue hospital gown. She would have hated the color. They let me stay with her for only a few minutes. I kept thinking her chest was moving. Kept expecting her to come to life and stroke my hair. Mostly I remember not being able to breathe. Crying so hard my face froze in a scream and I couldn't make a sound.

A hard knot formed in my throat. I paused to swallow it down.

"That morning she'd kissed me goodbye and told me not to forget my lunch. And by the afternoon she was dead. I went to sixth and seventh and eighth period, answering multiple choice questions about the Mayan Civilization and whatever the fuck, and sometime during all that my mom died, and I had no idea.

"We couldn't afford to live in our old apartment without two incomes. Even through all that, she worked, and a portion of her income still went to rent. Dad made sure of that—they had this joint fund that half her money went in directly from work, and I guess he changed the passcode or…" I waved my hand, still not looking up from the desk. "It's not important. Whatever, so we could afford the apartment when she was working. But she left no savings. So, after she died, we moved. Here, thirty miles away, where the houses were cheap. Dad transferred from being a real cop at a university to being a fake cop at a mall. And I...grew up. And that's my story."

I hung my head, but watched Billy closely. I needed to see his reaction. He was still, for a long while, eyes calculating. He put down his sandwich, and I thought I saw his hands shaking.

"Where...uh..." he cleared his throat. "I...I'm so sorry, Mo."

"Thank you."

"That's awful. I can't imagine your pain."

Yes. Sweet validation.

"Thanks."

"Um...yeah." He shuffled, then leaned on his elbows on Max's desk. "But where did you say you lived before here?"

"Boston. Well, Somerville." I rolled my eyes, smiling to keep the tears at bay. "Real Boston people get mad when you call Somerville 'Boston.'"

"Yeah. I remember." He pulled out a cigarette, rolled it in his fingers. "I used to live in Somerville."

"Oh, really?"

"Remember how I told you I ran away from my Grandma to the city?"

"Yeah. Because she hated your drums."

"Ha. Yeah, right. Well, I wasn't doing too hot when I got to there. I had no money. I crashed on the futon of a kid I knew from high school who was older. He'd already graduated. I was supposed to be a sophomore. Anyway, he shared an apartment in Somerville with six other guys. My first night there they gave me hydromorphone."

My throat tightened. "That's what Mom…"

He nodded, looking only at the cigarette.

"Like her, I got hooked. But I didn't have a job, and no one wanted me as their drummer. I needed money if I was gonna buy more pills. And they were the only guys who had it, at the time.

"So I started selling. That was their plan, you know… whatever.

"For two, three years I sold in the city. Climbed the ladder, got these tattoos, got into much harder drugs, started regretting it and wanting out. Eventually I got caught and to avoid jail time, I busted the gang—and, I mean, we *were* a gang, in everything but the name—and the cops gave me a second chance. I asked for witness protection, but long story short, they said I didn't need to go that far with it. I disagreed, but…whatever. They helped me cover my tracks, though. I ran out here, sobered up, got better."

Dude, I *called it* that he was in a gang, right from the moment I met him. My celebration was pretty short-lived, though. Because why else would he have brought up this story, specifically, if not for the fact…?

He went on. "But while I was selling…"

"Did you know Ronald?" I cut in.

He winced. "Um…" He paused, then nodded painfully. "I did. He was in my group. I'm sure it was the same Ronald. We were the only people selling hydromorphone in Somerville at the time."

My head flushed. I felt my breathing speed up. He *knew* Ronald.

"I don't know if this makes it better, or…but I do know we never meant to hurt anybody. Ronald didn't mean to hurt your mom. And our stuff was untainted."

I had a hundred questions, a hundred feelings, and mostly I just wanted to run.

"Was he…the friend you lived with?"

Billy paused again, running his thumb over his knuckles, then nodded with his eyes squeezed shut.

Fuck you, my brain shouted. I told it to shut the hell up.

"I lived with Ronnie a long time." *Ronnie.* "He wasn't even the worst of them, just a normal guy who got on a bad path. We lost clients all the time like how your mom went…it's easy to make a mistake with the dosage, especially on a relapse." He ran his hand over his nose. "What was your mom's name?"

I swallowed. "Amy."

He didn't react. I held my breath, staring fixedly on his every move, but I couldn't see a single emotion cross his face. I wanted him to say that it wasn't her, almost as much as I wanted him to say it was. Then, he took a deep, shaky breath.

"A mistake," he finally repeated, hardly louder than a whisper.

Ronald talked to him about my mom. He knew her—knew *about* her, anyway. I felt like I was going to pass out.

"A mistake." I took in a deep breath. "So maybe it wasn't…maybe it wasn't suicide, maybe she just made a mistake?"

Even though they (and you, probably) tell people not to blame themselves for suicide, it's hard not to. Because if I was a better daughter, maybe she wouldn't have killed herself, you know? So now, knowing that it was likely not suicide, for just a tiny moment, I felt a little better.

But then, my brain finished, *if it wasn't suicide, it was murder.*

I didn't bother to turn off that negative voice this time. I didn't want to. I couldn't breathe, and my head was swirling, and it was not a suicide, but not a mistake, either. Because if Ronald hadn't given her the drugs, she wouldn't have died.

So it's a murder.

My chest had finally relaxed, but now my stomach was boiling. Billy knew my mother's murderer. Billy may have murdered another person's mother. I called a drug-dealing murderer my friend. My only real friend.

And even *he* felt bad for me, by the way.

My head, my head, my *head.* I went to the bathroom and stayed there, staring at my reflection in the grimy mirror, trying to slow down my breath and my heartbeat, trying to think about Elise or Claire or school or anything else but my mom's dead face in the hospital bed, and Billy, five years younger, *knowing* the guy who did that to her.

You'd ask how I felt, in that moment, and I don't know. I felt *everything.* I felt sad and broken, and angry, and most of all confused and overwhelmed, and I wanted to drive my fist through the grimy mirror and never feel anything ever again.

Then I turned on the cold water full blast and kept my

hands there until I couldn't feel them, then splashed my face and held my cold, thin, shaking fingers to the back of my neck, and then just squatted down and stared at this cracking, seafoam green floor tile and completely broke down.

Not loudly. I'm good at keeping my crying quiet, because whenever Dad hears me crying, he comes in and wants to talk about it, and I never want to deal with that. I knew Billy would do the same now. So, when my body opened my mouth, I held in the scream and held my breath, and my lungs ached as they choked in air, and the tears fell all over my hot face. And tears fuzzed my vision, then fell onto the tile, and I felt frozen, and broken, and torrential.

Now I pressed my cold hands all over my forehead and cheeks and neck and eyes, but I knew not to wipe at my tears too hard.

After a while, I caught my breath and my composure. I rose up and looked at myself in the mirror. Not horrible. I took toilet paper (softer than paper towels) and dabbed at my undereyes gently. If you rub too hard, your eyes look more like you cried. I'm glad, in retrospect, that I'd stopped wearing so much eyeliner, because that would have made it super obvious. I breathed deep and used more cold water to cool down my skin, slow my breath.

Slow breaths. I had to look normal, and break is almost over. *Elise, think of Elise.*

It was hard. Super hard. All I wanted to do was scream and disappear forever.

I leaned against the bathroom door until the end of break, when it took all the courage in the world (and three or four attempts) to leave the bathroom. I then escorted bunny Billy back to his egg-shaped throne.

"I'm sorry," he whispered through the bunny suit as we walked. "I know, I have a lot to make up for." He sighed, then added, "A lot of bad karma. A lot."

I forced a smile and said it was fine. And that's how I decided I did, actually, have a right to complain about my life. And a right to be mad at Billy, even if he was only loosely connected to Ronald. And a right to be glad I'd never see his stupid, tattooed face again after Easter.

The next day, I had Kathi escort Billy to break. I stayed on set, staring at the second floor. Those guys who talked to my dad must have been the guys in his gang. I glared at the spot on the railing where the man in the hoodie leaned over to look at the bunny set, lollipop dangling from his lips. Something inside told me I was right in thinking that that man was Ronald.

Ronald was at my mall. He talked to my dad. He surveyed my place of work. And he killed my mom.

Slowly, my rage was overtaken by my fear.

What did he want with us?

Twenty-Two

On Feeling Bad

The next day at work, I could hardly keep my eyes open. I couldn't sleep the night before, because every time I closed my eyes I saw Ronald's face, his half-sucked lollipop, and got furious that that ugly, awful man handed Mom the very pills that did her in. I imagined screaming at him, beating him up, throwing him over the railing of the second floor to crash dead onto the pastel Easter-egg rug.

Then my mind would cycle into fear and paranoia. Because I knew I couldn't beat him up. I couldn't do a thing.

So basically, I was staying up all night, and since that was the case, I decided around three in the morning to give into it and distract myself with sewing, like I had been doing a month before when my dad, depression checklist in hand, asked if I had insomnia, like my mother had taught me to do.

"Never spend your time doing something unproductive," she said. This was when she was sober, I think. "If you must watch TV, do something creative at the same time."

She taught me basic painting, knitting, and origami, but what stuck was sewing. I inherited her machine and meager kit, which had since grown spectacularly. I'd gone through all her thread and I hardly ever use her machine (the dolls' size means hand sewing is actually easier), but I do still use her thimble, though.

See? She wasn't all bad.

But Billy, surely, was good, too. Despite his past.

Not Ronald, though. Ronald was all bad. I was sure of it.

Kathi held true on her promise to escort Billy to break, which was fine. She came back from break chattering about how nice he is, and about how she talked with him about how annoying her boyfriend's roommate is, something funny Billy said. Billy stared at me through the bunny mask as I nodded along to Kathi singing his praises.

Oh good, one part of my brain said sarcastically. *He's still racking up good karma. Good for him.*

He's being nice, another part countered.

He probably killed someone, a third part chimed in. *And even if we wanted to hang out with him again, could we even look at his face without seeing Ronald in those tattoos?*

He's a friend, said a fourth. *And I miss him. He's worth trying for.*

You know, one thing you didn't tell me was how to choose which voice to listen to when you're not sure which one is right.

Some space didn't feel like a bad thing, but I didn't want him to think things were broken permanently, so when I grabbed my bag from the break room to go home, I slipped the Bart Simpson doll I made last night into Billy's jacket. I had had enough yellow left over from the first Bart to make him a smaller one of his own, since he liked the photo so much. I figured he'd know it was from me, so I didn't leave a note.

I felt so mature in doing that. In avoiding discussion. In sweeping things under the carpet.

"It's so hard," I told you. "The brain thing. Listening to my brain and telling one part it's being too negative, and only listening to the good part—it's hard. Sometimes it's hard to even know which part is good and which part is bad."

"It is hard," you said. "But then again, noticing a thought is the first step in changing it."

You were wrapped up in this big chunky yellow sweater that looked pretty cozy. It was freezing in your room. When I first walked in you said I probably shouldn't take off my coat, because the office lost power last night and only got it back late in the morning, so the heat was still fighting to get going. So I was still in my coat and you were in your sweater. You had a steamy cup of tea, but it was almost not steaming anymore. I wanted to tell you that I wouldn't find it rude if you drank it while I was here, but I didn't for some reason.

You crossed your arms tight around yourself. "When was the last time you tried to do this?"

I didn't want to tell you about how I felt after Kathi talked with Billy. I figured you'd think I was being jealous of her getting to spend time with him, and I didn't feel like diving into the whole Ronald thing. So I told you about how Billy felt bad about my story, about my mom dying. I didn't mention how he knew Ronald, or how any of that was involved. I just told you what I thought you needed to know.

"My mind was happy that he felt bad for me. Because I've been trying to work out whether or not I deserve to feel bad about my own life. And if he feels bad for me, then I can, too. But I don't know—"

"Whoa, slow down," you said, smiling a little. "You think you don't deserve to feel bad about your life?"

"No, I think I do."

"But only because Billy sympathized with you."

"Well, he confirmed that I have had a tough life." I was embarrassed of those words before they even came out of my mouth. "Because if a guy like Billy feels bad for me, I *have* to have had it bad."

"What if he didn't sympathize with you? What if he just sort of nodded and said 'ooh, that's rough,' but didn't really mean it?"

That was what I was worried he would do. "Then I guess I would have been exaggerating."

"Do you think..." you gazed out the window a moment, in thought. "Do you think your emotions can lie to you? Can you ever be too happy about something?"

"Yeah. Like sore winners. Or when you think something is going to be better than it is."

"Mm. Well, so, you can express emotions poorly, sure. But when you feel happiness, do you think you're ever not *really* happy? When you laugh uncontrollably, do you ever wonder if the joke was *really* that funny?"

"Sometimes John makes stupid jokes I know shouldn't

be funny, but we laugh at them for a long time anyway." Usually when we're high.

"If you laugh, it's funny, right? Even if you know it shouldn't be, it's still funny."

"Yeah. Sure."

"So, if you feel happy, you're happy. No one can argue and say, 'No, you're wrong, you're not actually happy.'"

"Yeah…" I could see your conclusion ahead of time, and it filled me with knots.

"So if you feel sad, you're sad. It's impossible for someone to argue and say, 'No, you're not actually sad.' If you feel sad, you are."

"But you *can* argue and say you *shouldn't* be sad. Like, that commercial everyone was talking about last year, where the dog is abandoned and then is saved by a family on Christmas—it's a commercial, it's not real, and it's just trying to sell you chicken noodle soup, so you *shouldn't* be sad."

"But if you are, you are. 'Should' doesn't really…come into play."

"But it *does*."

"Who says?" you countered with this all-knowing smile, which was a little annoying. "You 'should' clean your room, because your dad wants you to, and you don't want ants. You 'should' come to class on time, because your teacher is taking attendance and you'll get a bad grade if you miss class, right? But who is the one telling you you 'should' feel this way or that?"

"Well, I don't think you should—" I grimaced, now annoyed at myself for using 'should.' "—I don't think you

should need someone else to tell you those things. You...
should want to come to class to learn. To benefit yourself, in
the future."

"Okay, so why *should* you not feel sad at the dog
commercial? Who does that benefit?"

I thought on that one for a long time. Maybe twenty
full seconds. "I don't know. Not really yourself, if you bottle
up your emotions. I guess it's just that you shouldn't be so
sensitive."

"Says who?"

"I don't know...how can you get through life if you cry
at dog commercials? How are you going to survive when
actual bad stuff happens to you?"

You nodded, let my own words sink in, then asked, "Do
you think you would have cried at the dog commercial when
you were a kid?"

"I was inconsolable at the end of *Charlotte's Web*," I said
with a little smile. "So, well, yeah."

"And today, you've already survived one of the worst
things that could happen to you."

A tiny little voice was excited, way in the back of my
head, to get more validation. "Yeah..."

"Do you think if you had toughened up and not cried
at *Charlotte's Web* that losing your mom would have been
any easier?"

"No. Definitely not."

"So...?"

I left your office frustrated, because what you said made
sense but I didn't think it should. And I was confused, too,
and worried, because I kind of wanted to tell you about

Ronald, but I didn't know how, and I was worried you'd have to tell the cops or my dad because I was maybe in danger. And I also kind of wanted you to have to do that, but I was scared of you having to do that. I don't know.

It was the same way I felt when my dad confronted me with a print-out of the top seven signs of depression, with five of them circled. I had wanted help, but I didn't want help, and I didn't want to be the one to ask for help, either. I hate feeling so conflicted, all the time, about *everything*. I just want my brain to make sense.

I had a date with Elise the next day, and was excited, despite the gnawing worry in my lower stomach over Ronald and Billy and "shoulds" and "should nots." She was, after all, the only completely good thing in my life.

I wanted to talk to Billy, maybe apologize for ditching him the last few days, and maybe tell him I don't think he's a bad person for what he did in the past. And maybe I'd ask him if he thought Ronald would hurt me, now that he found me. But Max escorted Billy to break today. I couldn't imagine Billy *not* sitting behind Max's desk, *not* smoking a cigarette. Fun break, I'm sure. Anyway, I didn't really get to talk to him.

And when Max got back, he was in a really good mood. Because Billy has that effect on people. Normal people, anyway.

Okay. So, the date. It was already supposed to be a short

date. It was a Tuesday, a school night for both of us, and she had a big, sophomore-in-college paper to write, so it was just supposed to be a quick dinner in the food court (with maybe a bubble tea afterward).

I waited for her on a bench by Pandora's Box. I'd just passed the first five levels of Blocki when a hunk of yellow fabric blocked my vision.

I'd stared at that color for hours two nights ago—it was the Bart plushie. What was Billy—

I craned my neck up, expecting Billy or the bunny, but saw Elise.

"Hey there, beautiful," she said.

I smiled, shoved my phone away. "No, you're beautiful."

"Oh, 'eat my shorts.'"

I popped up from the couch. "How'd you get Bart?"

"Billy gave him to me."

Tension dropped through my belly. "You know Billy?"

"I met him earlier today. He came into Pandora's Box and wandered around like the new kid on the first day of school. Smelled like a carton of cigarettes. My coworker Bethany went up to him to help and he said he was looking for 'a cute lady with glasses and dreadlocks whose name, I think, starts with an E.'"

Her impression was spot-on. We started walking slowly to the food court.

"Billy told me you made this for him, but you were afraid to tell me you made dolls—though, I can't imagine why, considering it's a really cool hobby and you're so good at it."

"Oh it's—it's just kinda dorky, and—"

"Okay, but I'm dorky, so, right up my alley."

"You're not dorky."

"You—" she smiled off past her shoulder, letting her arms fall to her sides. "You just don't know me well enough, yet. You saw my board game collection. And I have a bookcase, floor to ceiling, filled with manga. And not cool, action manga—high school romance manga. Sexy werewolf manga. Trust me. I *know* dorky. I *love* dorky."

"What! Where was that bookcase? I was in your apartment."

"In my room at home, at my parents' house. I was even too embarrassed to bring them to college, so I'm well aware of my dorkiness. And I *told* you, you regret what you don't say more than the things you do say, right? You ought to have told me. I wanna know everything about you."

She was so reassuring, so real. And so excited. Her hand was gently wrapped around the inside of my arm and I felt…like she was a messy, weird human like me, not some angel, for maybe the first time. Which is really unfortunate timing, because the next thing she said was, "So, where did you learn to sew?" and I said, "My mom taught me," and then for some reason she asked, "What else did your mom teach you?"

And it was a casual enough question. It wasn't meant to mean anything. And I could have said any number of things. My mom taught me painting. Knitting. Origami. But my dumb ass thought that because she accepted doll-making, she'd accept anything, so my dumb ass said:

"Shoplifting."

I said it in this sarcastic mumble. Maybe I was trying to seem as cool as I thought she was. Or maybe I was trying to be honest and share my stories like Billy was trying to teach me to do. I don't know.

But I said it. And she laughed, then said, "What?" in the same, half-serious voice.

I was panicking. I shrugged. She stopped walking, and her hand was still on my arm, so I stopped, too.

"Your mom taught you…shoplifting?"

"Yeah."

"Were you like, really poor? Like, you needed to, to survive?"

"No. Not even." I laughed, like, *isn't it crazy?* She did not join in, and the hints of compassion in her eyes vanished.

"Why, then?"

I sighed. "She was an addict. Opioid addict, and needed the money for her pills. I think the reasoning was that if *I* was caught, they would just report me to her, and we wouldn't get in any real trouble, whereas if *she* shoplifted and got caught it would be a much bigger *thing*. I was only thirteen."

"Oh, my god."

"Yeah, so, it's not like I would have gone to jail or anything, or even gotten fined, probably. Not that I ever got caught." I tossed my hair over my shoulder in sarcastic pride. She didn't think it was funny.

"I'm so sorry. What an awful thing…."

Elise released my arm to hug Bart to her chest. We took a few more steps. And I thought for a minute it was over.

That she was probably just sad that my *mother*, of all people, taught me something like that at such a young age. That Mom disillusioned me. It was like if Billy took off the bunny head in front of all the kids—it's sad when kids lose their innocence like that, and my mom definitely did that for me when she taught me shoplifting.

"What kind of things did you shoplift?"

She didn't think it was funny, or cool, or rebellious, or quirky, and for the first time, neither did I. It felt instead like I was admitting to some sort of crime.

"I don't know…everything, really. We started with bras. Then DVDs, earrings—"

"Bras?"

Oh, fuck. I could feel it coming, like how a dog senses a thunderstorm. The vision I had had of us becoming a gay Bonnie and Clyde, ripping off Pandora's Box together popped into my head and made me feel like an idiot.

But then I bristled. She should know, more than anyone, that stealing from a big company doesn't matter. The company can survive a small loss, and fuck capitalism, and everything else. She *should* agree with me.

So I took a breath and said, "Yeah, bras," and when she followed up with what I knew was coming: "Do you…still shoplift?" I rolled my shoulders back and said, "Yes."

She stopped walking again. At this rate we'd never make it to the food court. She squeezed Bart tightly, looking like a heartbroken little kid. "I fucking knew it. At my apartment, I could tell, I just didn't want to…" She shook her head bitterly. "You're not a C-and-a-half cup."

"Wh—"

"You were wearing two bras, the day we met, weren't you? When I measured you. I knew something felt off."

Some of my badassery and boldness evaporated. She was right. She caught me, and she could tell my father. She'd probably out me to him, in the process, and I wasn't sure which would make him hate me more. And she may never want to see me again, over the fact that I started our relationship off while stealing and lying to her. But then my anger doubled down again. She wasn't *listening* to me, wasn't getting it at all, and I was already *so* tired of having to defend my actions to Nora, and Claire and John, and Billy, and Dad, and *you*, honestly. I threw a hand up in the air.

"Oh, come on," I countered.

"What? You stole from Pandora's Box for no reason. For a free, expensive bra, right under my nose. *Literally.*"

"Yeah, so?" I scratched my nose violently. "It's just a bra."

"It's illegal."

"Illegal?" I dropped my voice. "Like egging a house? Like sneaking into Santa's fucking workshop?"

"That's different, you know it is. No one got hurt by us sneaking into the office, and—"

"Nora had to clean old, goopy eggs off her house. That sucks. We did that to her. A fifty-dollar bra that cost Pandora's Box twenty-five cents to make—thanks to their unpaid child laborers in God knows where—is not even half as bad. Stealing from a big business is a victimless crime. Egging is not. So, you don't really have the moral high ground. And by the way, you cooked stroganoff with stolen mushrooms, so your hands aren't as clean as you think they are."

God, why did I have to dig myself even deeper with that? I kept expecting her to cut me off, but she didn't. She just stared at me, Bart in a chokehold between her crossed arms, her face frozen in a frown.

I went on: "I mean, I don't even get why you care. Do you really feel bad for capitalist big businesses? Because that's not how I pegged you."

I waited. Eventually Elise took a big breath and finally said, in a low, controlled voice, "I didn't want to egg the house. I did it for you. I *thought* she had really hurt you, and was therefore not innocent. And you know what? If shoplifting only hurt the asshole CEO, or didn't hurt anybody, I *wouldn't* care. But you know who got in trouble for it? For you stealing that bra? The employees. Specifically, me. I got *screamed* at. My boss threatened to fire me if it happened again under my watch. That's why I was late for our first date—because I was getting yelled at for something *you* did." Her voice was rising, in pitch and volume and speed. She took another slow breath, her eyes closed, and when she spoke again her voice was quieter, calmer. "And I didn't suspect you for a second. God, I'm an idiot. Are you only dating me so you can steal more—"

Fuck, fuck—

"No, Elise—" I took a step forward, but she took a step back. That was what made me realize I might have fucked up, big time, and I felt a pull of worry in my stomach. "No, no, no, no, no, they're completely not connected. I really like you, and that has nothing to do with this."

She held out Bart, her eyes trained on him, not daring to look up at me. I took the doll from her, reluctantly.

"I'm a bit too old for this," she said, and for a minute I thought she meant the doll. "It's too black and white. You've got to see the nuance in the world."

So do you, my mind shot back, but I swallowed my pride and instead said, "I do," but even to my ears it sounded like a whine. "I…I'm sorry. You're right. I didn't think about the workers who—"

"You said it was a victimless crime," she said. "But it's not. You're right, you're not hurting the corporations. Not at all. The only people you're hurting are retail people like me, like me and the stupid cashier at the supermarket and who knows who else you stole from. You've probably gotten a lot of poor people yelled at. Maybe even fired. Didn't you ever stop to think about them?"

"What, the college kids?" I said, not meaning to call her out. *Shut up, Mo, shut up shut up shut up,* I thought, but my mouth was moving faster than my mind.

"The poor people. In poverty. Single parents?"

"It's mostly college kids."

"Oh my God!" she said, with a touch of incredulous laughter. "No, it's *not!* Look around you, Mo, the mall isn't just staffed with college kids. And look, even if it was, they don't deserve to get yelled at. *I* didn't deserve to get yelled at."

My anger flared up again. "I'm sorry, okay, that you got *yelled* at, but it really wasn't the end of the world."

"They threatened to fire me."

"But they *didn't.*"

"But they *could* have. And nobody deserves to get fired just so you can have a fancy bra you don't need for free. Even if I'm not poor and could get a different job, and I didn't end up getting fired—you caused me pain, for no reason, and you don't even feel bad about it!" Elise took a sharp breath as if she were going to continue, then closed her eyes and pressed the air out her nose.

Well, it wasn't for 'no reason' you got yelled at, part of my brain bickered. *You* didn't *catch me. I successfully shoplifted from you. It's your fault, for not doing your job right.*

Stop, I told myself, but it just kept going. *Stop,* I insisted. *Focus. What thought do I want to focus on?*

I fucked up, another part of my brain piped up. *I'm sorry.*

"I'm sorry," I tried aloud. "I really do like you, and…I can stop. I *will* stop. I'm sorry."

"How am I supposed to believe that? How am I supposed to believe anything you tell me? You've been lying to me since the moment we met." She waited for me to respond, but I had no idea what to say. I looked down to avoid her eyes. She sighed again. "I gotta go. I think we're done."

"Elise—"

"No. I think we're done."

Twenty-Three

Breakthrough

She left me.

It sounds dramatic to say it like that.

It also sounds dramatic for me to have cried all night. We had only been on a handful of real dates. I could picture every single different outfit I have ever seen her wear. We were basically nothing. But she was the first person I'd ever really dated. The first person I'd ever slept with. The first person I'd ever felt so comfortable and happy with. She was the first something I'd ever had.

It felt like she'd ripped out some of my intestines. So much for "I want to know everything about you," huh?

You already know how hard it was for me, because I spent the next session with you in tears over her.

"I shouldn't even *be* crying," I told you, crying.

You handed me another tissue, then said "Here," and handed me the whole box. I kind of smiled through my tears at you. The tissues came back gray, stained by mascara. I could only imagine what my face looked like.

"Why do you say that?" you asked.

"It was such a short thing." I blew my nose in the tissue.

"Maybe. But she obviously meant a lot to you."

"Yeah, but. It's not like she died. I shouldn't be so sad and…snotty."

"No, you're right. She didn't die. But that doesn't mean you're not allowed to feel emotions about her. That doesn't mean this doesn't hurt."

I didn't say anything to that, because it was hard to articulate all my thoughts out loud in the moment, but here's what I was thinking: I was thinking that you were right. I was doing the "should" thing again. It *did* hurt, and that frustrated me, because if I was allowed to cry over the end of a relationship that hadn't even gotten started yet when there were people going through divorces and grieving the deaths of their loved ones, that meant I was wrong about Nora, too. Or else, like Claire said, I was a hypocrite who thought no one else's suffering ever came close to mine.

Maybe I did feel like that—even to the point where I was getting upset at my *own* emotions and saying even *they* didn't come close to the suffering I underwent in the past. And maybe I really was as bad as Elise seemed to think I was.

You furrowed your brow a bit, then leaned forward, your elbows resting on your knees. "Mo, you are a very bright, very complicated young woman who is dealing with emotions so big and heavy even adults would be crippled by them—but you are not crippled by them. You are holding your head up high, and marching through like a warrior."

Yeah, sure. I snorted. "More like a guerrilla soldier, hurting everyone she comes across."

You paused. You do that a lot, waiting for me to say

more. Even though I know you're doing it, I fall for it quite often—but not today. You waited, and when you realized I wasn't going to add anything else, you went on.

"Do you think there is any way to reconcile with some of the people you feel you have hurt?"

And for the rest of the hour, we worked out a plan that, while difficult, would actually—probably—work.

I mulled over our plan all Thursday, which was my day off work, and Friday, during which I pawned Billy's break off on Kathi again. He lingered by me when they came back from break, but I just smiled and didn't catch his eye through the bunny mask. I wasn't ready to talk to him yet, and I figured it would be better after the plan. I was busy all through work, really planning the details, the dialogue with Dad in my head. I even planned during break, playing Blocki on autopilot, alone in Max's office. I took the opportunity to sit in Max's chair, and felt a bit betrayed that it was so comfortable and I had been balancing on a metal stool this whole time.

When I got home, I paced in my room, from my closet oak doors bursting with stolen merchandise to my window, complete with un-egged AC unit. I read over my plan, my script, my lists, and began worrying and freaking out and crying. I knew I had to do it. I just had to. But fuck, it sucked to think about.

I wasn't crying when Dad came home around eleven on Friday night, though I still felt congested from all my crying earlier in the day. I was sitting cross-legged on my bed, black-and-white checkered comforter bunched up behind me, busy finishing up the lists in the back of my Modern World History notebook. The final touches of my plan for a giant apology.

"Hey! You're still awake?" Dad said, appearing in my door frame. "Hey, I know it's not your favorite, but your grandmother was asking about it, so...you're still planning to come to church Sunday, ri—wait." His undereyes creased in worry. "Were you crying?"

I closed my notebook. "Um. Yeah."

My chest seized in fear, fluttering airy nerves. How on earth was I going to word this without him completely freaking out?

He sat next to me on the edge of my bed and took my hands in his. "What's going on, sweetie? You know you can tell me anything."

I nodded, but knew he was wrong. I lose a few pounds and mention I'm having trouble sleeping and he throws me in therapy (I'm glad, now that I went, but you have to admit it was an overreaction). I had no idea what he'd do when he found out I was shoplifting—and had been, for years, at *his* mall. Should I tell him I learned it from Mom? Should I give up the plan and never come clean, and just hope Elise doesn't rat on me?

And lose Elise?

Then I remembered you, and your calm office, and how we worked out a solution that would apologize to Elise and make up with Billy at the same time, and how even if they don't accept the apology they will know that *I* now know that I was wrong, about the shoplifting and about policing other people's emotions and experiences. That last part was your phrasing, but I adopted it here because I can't figure out how to word it any better. That's what I was doing—I was basically judging and punishing people, including myself, who I deemed were exaggerating or overreacting to their pain. But just because no one died doesn't mean emotions didn't happen. And just because the emotions weren't at a ten out of ten doesn't mean they're not worthy of acknowledgement. And someone doesn't have to die for a situation to result in a ten out of ten emotion. And that's okay.

That's so stupid, my brain said when I wrote that. *So cheesy.*

And I tried just now, like you told me, to thank my brain and follow a more positive thought instead, but it's still hard to do that. Whatever. I know what I'm doing is right, whether my full brain agrees with it or not.

I still felt awful, though. Because while it's good, I guess, that I was growing and accepting all this, I was *still* being selfish. I wasn't thinking of the retail employees, or how Dad would feel. I was only focused on the effect it would have on *me,* and the realization that even after all this I was still being selfish clutched around my chest in an icy fist.

I just stared at Dad while tears built up in my eyes, and before long he noticed and went to hug me. I was crying then, and Dad held me as I convulsed into tears, ugly tears, like the ones I used to cry over Mom.

"I'm an awful person," I choked out. Snot ran out my nose and over my lips. Tears exploded, goopy and hot. The more upset I got the more ashamed I became, of myself and of my pity party.

You probably would have said that even these emotions were valid and worth feeling, even if they were still centered on me. And I listened to you in my head like you were Jiminy Cricket.

That's so stupid, my brain fought back. *You are so fucking stupid.*

Dad was a trooper. He held me and tried not to ask too many questions. He told me he was here and he loved me, no matter what was going on, and I savored those words, because the part of me that kept telling me everything was stupid didn't believe him yet.

He hugged me close and I could smell the woodsy pine of his shampoo, and I remembered Mom's funeral. He had hugged me close then, too, and comforted me, even though he must have felt equally as awful.

Unlike me, Dad's always putting others first. Doing all he can for me, devoting all his time to others' safety. And even beyond that, he's always helping people move and jumpstart their cars and whatever. I shook with a sob into Dad's shoulder. *Fuck.*

I followed in the wrong footsteps.

Eventually, I could breathe again, and Dad, rightfully, asked what was going on. I gulped a few times and thought it over while he told me, again, that he wouldn't be mad, but that he had to know what was going on so he could help fix it.

Then my dad said, "I promise. I'm your dad. I can help you fix anything. And I want to help you."

I breathed a moment more. I thought I knew where to start.

"I feel so dumb for crying so much."

"Well, that's silly." He smiled, brushed new tears out from under my eyes. "Very smart people cry all the time."

"But it's like—I feel like I'm overreacting?"

He considered that for a moment. "Well, if this is all about Modern World History—" he gestured at my notebook. "—some would argue nothing is more deserving of tears." That got me to smile a little. After another pause, Dad went on. "I think people can only overreact if they're acting. Your mom used to overreact when I asked her to stop using those pills. She wasn't really that mad, she was just trying to get me to give in. But you're here, crying, and…well, I don't know why you're crying, but I don't think it's an act. It looks pretty honest to me."

Then I've got you fooled, that stupid part of my brain said, and for a minute it made me wonder if I really was faking it, for my dad's and my own pity. But I was getting better at recognizing that stupid part of my brain and knowing that it was wrong, thanks to your advice (thank you).

Noticing a thought is the first step in changing it, you said once. And I think I'm getting better, but I know I still have a long way to go. I can notice them, but they're still hard to ignore.

"I'm gonna tell you part of it," I said. He nodded. "So, I had just begun seeing somebody. A…an employee at Pandora's Box." Deep breath. Push through the nerves. You can't avoid pronouns forever. *Just do it. Just do it. Just say it.* "But…she dumped me."

"She dumped you?"

He didn't skip a beat.

So that's how I came out to my dad. I had been so worried over that for so long. I'd been so angry at the out-and-proud kids with supportive parents because I figured my Republican, cop dad would stop loving me if he knew. But he didn't. Not even for a second.

I couldn't bring that up just then, but later, I told him how much I appreciated it.

"Yeah," I said, wiping my nose on the back of my wrist, heart thrumming in my ears. "She did. Because I was a bad person, really, and—"

"Wait. You're a person," he said. "You may have done a bad thing, maybe, but that doesn't make you a bad person."

Yes, it does, I thought, but I wasn't sure who I believed.

"Well, then, I did a bad thing. And it made me realize that I'm selfish—"

"That you acted selfishly," he corrected. I had to bite back my frustration.

"Okay. I'm a person who did a bad thing and acted selfishly. Doesn't that make me a bad, selfish person?"

"No. It makes you a person who has not made all perfect choices. But you aren't a bad person who can't ever be good again." He gave a small smile at the blanket. "Your mom taught me that."

I considered. I hadn't *considered* Dad in a long time. I remember, when we lived in the city, imagining him as a knight defending the palace of the university. Then, after Holly-Marie Johnson said I didn't know what it was like to worry over my dad's life because he wasn't a *real* cop, like her dad was, I kind of stopped wondering, stopped considering.

And I guess I just kind of figured Dad wouldn't understand my problems because he's my dad, my dad who's always overprotective and…you know, *my dad*. I thought my problems would be too little, too under the radar, because he only notices the big signs, the five-out-of-the-top-seven symptoms of depression. After all, "real" cop or not, he was in the "real world," with taxes and mortgages and real things to worry about, while I was just some kid in high school, right? But I'm starting to realize that nobody can accurately tell an emotion's significance except the person having that emotion. And if I say it's real, and painful, then it's real and painful. And if my dad is really as smart as he seems to be, then he's already understood that fact for years.

And I need to get out of my head. And I need his help.

"I acted selfishly," I said, and before I realized what I was saying, this shot out of my mouth: "I had a fight with Nora."

Dad raised his brows. "Is Nora the girl you're…?"

"Oh! No," I said, though I honestly would have liked that to have been true, in another world. "She's *very* straight. This is another thing. A separate thing."

"Okay."

"She was complaining about her parents, which she does a lot. And I basically told her she doesn't have a right to complain, because at least her parents are both alive."

He paused. "Do you believe that?"

"I did, but I don't now. Or, I'm trying not to believe it, but it's hard to change my own mind. Elise, who's the girl I'm seeing—*was* seeing, I guess—told me I only think about myself and I don't know who I'm hurting. I think maybe I hurt Nora. And maybe I shouldn't get to decide who has the right to complain and who doesn't. Maybe everyone does. Maybe no one does, because someone always has it worse, right? But, maybe, since no one technically has the right to complain, that means *everyone* does." I took a quick breath. "And by 'right to complain,' really, I mean 'right to feel pain.' 'Right to feel bad about something,' and 'right to discuss those feelings.' But now—and with my therapist—I think everyone is 'allowed' to feel whatever emotions they feel, you know? I mean, how could I tell them they're wrong for what they feel? It's just hard for me to do that. But I'm trying, now."

Dad thought again. I was inspired by his slowness. He let every word sink in before responding.

I noticed a little mole behind his jaw, below his ear. I realized I might not have really *looked at* my dad in a long time, only seeing him in half-formed glances that my mind filled in the blanks on.

"You've gone through something awful, with Mom dying," Dad said, finally.

"You have, too."

"Yeah…" He nodded, sucking his teeth. "But that said, I don't think the spectrum of emotions is so…one or the other. Surely, you've been stressed out by a test or sad about something else. That doesn't mean you feel as bad as you did during the funeral, but you still feel bad, right? You feel bad right now, right?"

He rocked into me. Despite myself, I laughed.

"Yeah, I feel pretty bad right now," I said, smiling at my lap.

"Maybe you have a point," he said. "If Nora said she wished her parents were dead, or that she felt she had the worst life on earth, I'd say you would be right to roll your eyes at that. But complaining, even about small things? That's…human. And she probably did feel pretty awful when you told her she was wrong to feel the way she was feeling. And maybe she was mad about chores or something that doesn't seem serious to us, even if it is to her—but we don't know what it's like for her behind closed doors, either. Trust me when I say that some kids actually *would* be better off if their parents were dead."

He said this with a weathered weariness that made me realize that maybe being a university cop wasn't all guarding doors and confiscating bongs.

"I want to fix something," I said. "Actually, I want to fix a lot of things, but there's one thing I need to do tonight, and I need your help. But you can't ask questions about it, okay?"

"O…kay?" he said, probably expecting to just give me a ride to Nora's so I could apologize, or something.

And that's how I got my mall-cop dad to help me return thousands of dollars of stolen merchandise to the Carlindale Mall.

Twenty-Four

Saying Sorry

Dad was quiet as I opened my closet and started bringing everything out, spreading it out on the floor. It took more than ten trips. He watched, not touching any of it, and I kind of felt like I was putting on a weird, one-person play.

Bras, of course. DVDs, still in plastic wrap. Novelty mugs. Candles. Jars of jam, probably expired. Books. Paintbrushes. Three-packs of socks. Phone cases. Shorts, shirts, bikinis, underwear, tights, flip flops, hand towels. Little travel containers of shampoo. Reading glasses. Salt and pepper shakers. Sticky notes. Pens. Cat-shaped erasers. Spatulas. Mascara, blush, expensive makeup brushes. Hair ties. A universal TV remote. Headphones. Earrings. Nail polish. Nail clippers. Notebooks. Guitar picks. Fabric. Sewing needles. Scissors. Thread. Contact lens cases. Water balloons. Money clips. Alien stickers. Keychains. Batman figurines. The list goes on. After I dug it all out, I popped my phone case off, the one with red and orange ladybugs, and added it to the pile.

Dad stared at the sea of objects in front of him. I wondered how many of these things he recognized as having come from the mall. I had stuff from outside the mall too, of course, but I left that stuff in my closet to deal with another day. Besides, it was bad enough as it was, and my dad's worry lines already looked so tense they might start cutting off circulation.

"I have to give this stuff back to the mall," I said.

He raised his eyebrows and let out a big poof of air, his lips inflating out past his teeth. "What store is all this from? Gotta be more than one, right?"

That was technically a question, and he had promised he wouldn't ask questions, but I knew this wasn't the time to push it.

"More than one, yeah." I stepped over a pile to reach my Modern World History notebook and flipped it open to the back page. "I made a list of all the stores here."

We sorted things from my closet out by store. Like I mentioned before, I didn't usually use the stuff I took, so a lot still had tags (normal tags are safe. It's only those plastic security tags you'd have to watch out for) and were therefore easy to sort. The pile that didn't have tags and that I wasn't sure about was small.

Then there was the little egg frame I took from the Easter set. That was going to suck. I didn't take that with me. I figured I'd just give it back tomorrow morning, at work.

We put all the stuff in paper grocery bags and loaded up Dad's car. The ride over was quiet, Dad's country music playing so softly I could hardly hear it. I knew I was in trouble, but I wasn't really worried about that.

It was late, and the mall had been closed for over an hour, but the streetlamps were still on in the expansive parking lot, creating an eerily empty landscape you might see in an apocalypse film. Dad pulled right up to the front entrance and parked in the closest non-handicapped spot. It was the closest I had ever parked to the entrance.

With his keys, we got into the mall. He turned off the alarm system, then we left a bag of unstolen goods in front of each of the fourteen stores I had stuff from. It took a few trips out to the car and back into the mall, Dad unlocking and relocking the front doors every time. Part of me kept noting how easy it would be for Dad to unlock the doors to each store, for us to take more stuff right now. Old instinct, like how I found myself taking pictures of the beautiful chrysanthemum displays at Mom's funeral with the intent to show Mom later, since they were her favorite flower. I quieted my thoughts and focused on the task at hand.

Last on our list was Pandora's Box. I hadn't exactly planned it that way, but it was poetic. I dropped the big bag of bras out front, then dug in my backpack.

"Can we go inside this one?"

Dad shook his head. "If we leave them inside the store, they'll know someone on security was—"

"I know, but…" I dragged out the Bart Simpson doll—his face needed a little reshaping, poor thing. "It's for the girl I'm seeing. I want to leave it by her podium."

Dad glanced at the doll, then at me, then sighed, not unkindly, and—after finding the right key—lifted up the big garage-like, rolling doors. They jangled and squeaked, so loud in the empty mall.

We wandered inside, just us and a dozen headless and half-naked mannequins. I headed right over to Elise's podium by the changing rooms and settled Bart inside it, next to her measuring tape. I adjusted his little arm so it was poking out over the top edge of a stack of notebooks, kind of like he was waving. It was cute. A little creepy, I guess. But cute.

There was also a letter tucked up in Bart's shirt, addressed to Elise. In it, I explained what I'd done and said I'd give everything else back too, if I could. That I was done hurting other people, as much as I could help it. I wrote that I missed her and was so sorry, and if she could give me the tiniest chance, I would try to make it up to her, so I could deserve her. It was the best I could do, really. I rewrote it half a dozen times, but it still didn't feel good enough.

Dad (who hadn't said more than twenty words since we left the house) spoke up.

"So, this is where your girlfriend works?"

I winced. *Ex-girlfriend, I guess,* I thought. I recovered and ran my hand over the podium. "Yeah. Well, she worked here the day I met her, at least. She might not be at the changing rooms all the time. I don't know."

Now that all the bags were gone, Dad stretched out his back with a deep sigh, then stared around the red and black jungle of Pandora's Box.

"So…I know I said I wouldn't ask questions, but all that stuff was stolen, wasn't it?"

"Yeah," I said, because what else could I do? It was pretty obvious, and no lie would make sense. Besides, I was kind of done making excuses about shit.

"I knew your mother had a habit of it, sometimes."

"She brought me with her, sometimes," I admitted.

"Mm. I'm sorry she did that." He looked down at the

floor, kicked at the edge of a chipped tile. "She was such a good person. But those pills really…I'm sorry."

He was quiet for another long while, then, hands on his hips, said, "You know, I try to be a good police officer. A lot don't, but I do. And because of that, I don't believe in punishment for the sake of…revenge, or catharsis. It looks to me like you've already suffered some natural consequences, and made it as right as you could, returning all this stuff. I don't think it will be news for you if I were to tell you 'stealing is wrong.'"

Dad does his research, by God. He could probably write a full dissertation on his philosophy of *not* making children finish what's on their plate, if they're not hungry. His openness made him a good dad. And a good person. All the time.

"Let's just say I'm grounded?" I suggested. "I'll go to school, work, then right home. Help me break the habit and I don't get off scot-free."

"That works for me. I'll make some calls and tell the crew some excuse in the morning so when this is reported it doesn't end up on 7 News. I'll think of something."

"Thank you, Dad."

He hugged me for a long time.

"I just want you to be okay," he said in a whisper into my hair. "I want you to find a little joy. You deserve a little joy."

I wasn't sure if I did. I still felt like a bad person, not, in his words, just a person who made some bad decisions. But I'm working on it.

I hope "working on it" is good enough.

"Just try to find your joy legally, next time, okay?" he said, pulling back with a smile. I laughed. The tension lessened for the first time all night. "Can we agree on that?"

"Yeah. Of course."

He slung his arm around me and we walked out of the store, closing and locking the metal gates behind us.

Twenty-Five

Plans

It was over, and Dad and I were in the car, but I had no idea what to say. I mean, how do you *end* a fight when nobody storms off, like Elise and Nora did?

It wasn't even a "fight." More of an, "I admitted to doing a stupid, wrong thing, and now I know, despite his unconditional love, he's obviously a bit disappointed in me" kind of thing. But regardless, I just kind of sat in the front seat, watching the glare of the mall's streetlights haze up into the foggy night sky. It didn't feel right to pull out Blocki, even though I wanted to, so I just watched the town go by.

A new worry bubbled up in my head. "Will they even want all that stuff back?"

"Eh, I'll talk to some people," Dad said. "They can probably add a lot of it to their inventory, and the stuff they can't sell, well, we'll donate."

Silent again.

Dad smiled at the road, turned up the radio just a bit.

When we got back home, I ate a whole plate of leftover pasta. I hadn't finished a whole plate of anything in months.

Everything felt like it was coming to a close. I had nerves rumbling in my stomach over Elise's reaction to it all, but I felt like my part was done. The ball was in her court, and whatever happened, happened.

And if this was a movie, it would end there. But obviously, as you know already, it wasn't so easy.

One last day with the bunny. One last day before Easter. One last day for me to apply everything you and I worked through to Billy, because after Saturday I'd probably never see him again.

I had the next day planned out so perfectly. I would go in early, drop off my bag quickly, then find Elise and explain all of it. I would apologize and tell her that even if she doesn't want to take me back and give me a second chance that I was changing, and I wasn't shoplifting anymore. And hopefully she'd smile and hug me and tell me she was happy to see that I had seen the error of my ways. And then after my shift I planned to say goodbye to Billy and Kathi and Max. I'd tell Billy I was sorry for avoiding him and that I forgave him for selling drugs to people like my mom. I'd tell him he gets all the good karma, because he's a good person now, and we'd exchange phone numbers and hug, and maybe plan to meet up for lunch sometime in the future. Then I'd go over to Nora's (which I guess would go against my being grounded, but you can't knock all the rebel out of a person at once). Maybe she'd be outside cleaning the remaining egg off her car, and I would have to apologize for that, too. And maybe she wouldn't forgive me. But I'd apologize anyway, and then I'd apologize for telling her that her problems weren't bad enough to complain about, because everybody's pain is painful and everybody struggles, even if it doesn't seem like it. And just because I felt like I had it worse didn't mean that she didn't also have it bad, and everything else you and I talked about. Maybe Nora would forgive me, maybe not. But if she did, then maybe we could all hang out in Claire's treehouse again like normal, and we could smoke and I could tell Nora about my Easter Bunny job, and then maybe she'd finally feel comfortable enough to actually tell us why she hates her parents. And maybe it would seem really awful and maybe it wouldn't, but I wouldn't judge her. I would listen, and be considerate and compassionate and everything you are to me when I talk about all my problems, even though you probably hear a lot worse stuff every day at your job. And then, in a few weeks when I'm not grounded but still have money from the Easter Bunny job, I would take Claire, John, Nora, and Elise out for a big friends dinner where Elise could meet all my friends, and they'd all get along, and everything would be awesome.

God, I had so many plans.

And they were all fucked up by Ronald.

Twenty-Six

Actually, the "going in early to apologize to Elise" part was ruined by Max, to be specific. Because it was Saturday, the last day before Easter, the last day of the bunny, and he had me in at open for the first time. I figured I could set up whatever needed to be set up and then sneak off to Pandora's Box for a minute, but Max wasn't there to ask yet, and when he did finally burst in like a hurricane, I knew he wouldn't be having it.

Kathi was there, too, bright and early, hunching in front of Max's giant mirror and blending her makeup with one of those butt-plug-shaped sponges. She and I sipped coffees in mildly comfortable silence while we waited for Max. Billy came in first, already in costume (except for the head), and pulled over a metal chair to sit beside me. I kind of nodded at him and he nodded back, and I really wanted to talk but didn't want to talk in front of Kathi. I also didn't want to give the frame (which was burning a hole in my pocket) back in front of Kathi. She was just too much of a stranger.

Max burst in not long after, saving us all from the awkwardness. He began pacing and was already sweating—more than usual.

"Okay," he said, and we all looked up to him. "None of you have ever worked a Santa set. Easter never gets as popular as Santa, except for today. Everybody and their mother will be here, and the more little shits we get on Billy's lap, the more money we all make. It's the last day on set, but the first day in hell. So I hope you're ready."

I thought he was exaggerating, but he wasn't. There was already a line outside, waiting for the doors of the mall to open—which was also why, apparently, Billy had to be in the chair *before* the doors opened. Otherwise, Max said, there would be a riot. I also figured this wasn't an exaggeration.

I offered to escort Billy down. He popped the head on while still in the office, just in case a mall employee brought their kid to work. Wouldn't want to traumatize the poor things.

They'd get traumatized enough, soon.

I thought of Elise's cute little niece, Brayden. I was hung up on Elise, annoyed that I wouldn't get the chance to see her before work. I couldn't leave Billy on set alone, and I wasn't on good enough terms with him at the moment to ask if we could detour—nor did we have the time. I'd just have to swing over on break, or after my shift. No biggie. I guess.

Billy and I exited the service hallway and we passed the security office (which my dad would be unlocking any moment now) then turned the corner to pass the diamond store. Out in front of a few stores we passed—most hadn't opened, yet—were my bags of unstolen things. My stomach clenched. My dad was already here, and hopefully he'd be able to calm everyone down about them when they started freaking out. I shook my head. One thing at a time.

We were about to pass the pet store's Easter rabbit display when I finally worked up the nerve to speak.

"So…I don't know if I should thank you or punch you."

"Oh yeah?" Billy's voice was muffled from the bunny head.

"For giving Bart to Elise."

"What did she say?"

The bunny head turned to me with its awful perpetual smile. Behind the mask I saw Billy's eyes, but his emotion was indecipherable.

"Well…it led—and I'm still not quite sure how—to me admitting to shoplifting. And she was so mad."

"Yeesh."

"Yeah. So, I gave all of it back to the mall. In hopes that she'd forgive me."

"What do you mean, 'all' of it?"

"All of it. Piles and piles. Hundreds, maybe thousands of dollars. Everything I ever took from the mall—except the food, I guess. And some of the fabric and thread and such, because…well… And this, yet," I said, holding up the frame. I gave it to him, and he took it, turning it over in his bunny paw. "But I did my best. Long story short, my dad knows and I'm grounded. But whatever." I took a nice, clear breath. "Thing is, I feel a lot better."

His eyes smiled. "That's awesome, Mo."

We turned a corner and the set came into view. It finally hit me that this was the last time, probably ever, that I would go to work here, and I caught a bit of that nostalgic sadness I had whenever an older friend graduated. The same nostalgic sadness I'd been feeling all year at my *last* homecoming, my *last* pep rally, my *last* holiday talent show.

Then I immediately felt bad for feeling sad about something so unimportant, and then, again, reminded myself that it was okay to feel things on a spectrum, like you and my dad and everyone keep trying to tell me. I was getting frustrated at how slow my mind was to learn this. I *knew* it was true, so why didn't I believe it yet? I guess it was just going to take practice. But it will be worth it, I think. I never noticed, until you all pointed it out, how negative I was. How judgmental, of myself and everyone else.

"I'm gonna tell Max later," I said as I took the frame back from Billy.

"Hope he doesn't fire you," Billy said in a sarcastically worried tone. "Well. Seems like giving Bart to Elise kind of worked out."

I realized I had never seen him fully out of the bunny suit, and probably never would. I stared at him as we walked, trying to take in a real good mental picture. The Easter season flew by.

"Kinda. So, thank you, I guess. I hope your stuff also works out. The karmic rebalancing. The tattoo removal."

His tone brightened. "That should, anyway! I have an appointment in two weeks."

I smiled, shoved my hands in my back pockets.

"Hey, we never got a chance before," I said. "But if you ever wanna give me drum lessons—"

"Oh, I'd love to," he said, then added, "I'm smiling. If you can't tell."

"I can."

At that moment, I kind of knew we'd never play music together. Just like how I knew the graduating seniors wouldn't come back to visit "all the time." But even though I knew it probably was goodbye forever, making the plans softened the blow a little. I let us both have a softer blow, and I'm glad I did.

We passed the pet store, MakeAlive Cosmetics, Macy's. Macy's was open; they had probably already seen my bag of "returns" and were adequately puzzled by it. I knew it was safe, since Dad would take care of it later, but it was still weird knowing what must be going through the retail workers' minds.

I figured I'd get through my last shift, say goodbye to Billy, Max, and Kathi, then head down to apologize to Elise, who would more than certainly put two and two together before I got there.

All I had to do was make it through hell first.

Twenty-Seven

The Spare

"Oh, god, look at that line," I said.

We could see the locked, glassy front doors of the entryway from here, beyond the bunny set. The line was more like a crowd, going back off the sidewalk in all directions, filled with parents, strollers, and a million little kids, all dying for a chance to meet Billy.

"Holy shit," Billy whispered. He stopped dead in his tracks, took two shaky steps back, then full-on sprinted in the opposite direction.

It took a moment for what just happened to click in my mind. I stood dumbfounded for a second, then laughed dumbly, then an uneasiness spread through my body.

"Billy?!"

He didn't turn back so I ran after him, but he was way faster. He banged a right at the fork and disappeared—I thought down a hall to the left, but he could have easily slipped into one of the shops, or another service hallway. When we used to play hide and seek in the mall, this area was one of the best places to get to once they saw you. There were a million places to run off to. I groaned. I knew he didn't have his phone on him. Why the hell did he take off like that? The kids would be in any minute; we had to get him in his seat.

"Billy!" I called. Someone folding clothes in a kids' clothing store looked up, but as they weren't a six-foot Easter Bunny, I paid them no mind.

"Mo?"

I whirled around. Elise. She was holding the bag of bras in one hand, Bart in the other. She wore an indecipherably emotionless, flat line of a mouth.

Shit. I was not ready for this moment, for this big apology. I was not prepared for *any* of this. I stared at her, then at the bag, which she hiked up higher on her hip.

"So, obviously you—" Elise began, but then I saw Max and Kathi heading out of the service hallway—which meant Billy wasn't in that hallway, which meant he was either in the kids' clothing store, that breakfast place, the pet store, the security office—well, that wouldn't make sense—or maybe he *did* go down that other hallway and hit the bathroom? Maybe his *"shit"* was literal?

"I'm sorry, Elise, I'm so sorry, I have to go. I lost the bunny." I took a few steps toward Max and Kathi, everything in my body telling me to stay with Elise. I looked back at her. "I'm sorry."

Her eyes narrowed. "You lost the—"

"Later, I promise, we'll talk later."

She watched me go.

Max and Kathi were bringing down two big bags of those awful, cheap chocolates. Max's eyes went wide when he saw me, and he launched right into panic mode.

"Billy ran off when he saw the crowd," I said, then

added, "Stage fright, or maybe he got diarrhea, I'm not sure."

Max pulled his lips into his mouth. "You're kidding."

"I don't know; I don't know where he went. He just ran off. I couldn't catch him; he either went down this way or out that way," I said, gesturing to the hall in the opposite direction. "Or into one of the shops or something."

Max stared at the opposite hallway, calculating. There was no way to search everywhere quickly enough.

Then Max pointed his oily, thin finger at me and said, "Put on the spare bunny suit."

I felt all the blood flush out of my head. "What?"

"We don't have time for Billy's bullshit, especially if we don't even know where he is. Kathi, you get down to the set." He loaded his bag of candy on top of hers, blocking her view. "Answer questions and hold back the crowd until we get there. We probably won't make open."

She turned sideways and grapevined down to set, looking like a fashionable soccer player with an affinity for bad chocolate.

"Come with me."

Max took off toward the service hallway at a run. I followed close behind, mind whirring. Billy was probably in the bathroom. But why didn't he just say to me, "Oh, I need the bathroom?"

Max and I burst into his office. Billy's bag and clothes were still there, but Billy wasn't. That meant he probably didn't leave the mall, since his car keys were here.

"Ohh, goddammit, Billy, goddammit goddammit," Max sighed in a singsong voice laced with aggravation. He pulled the spare suit off the rack and tossed it to me. "Get changed," he said, then left the room to give a semblance of privacy.

The back-up suit was horrible. *Bright* pink, head to toe, dead-looking black ovals for eyes, giant buck teeth that nearly reached over its chin. No clothes, like Billy's cute blue vest—just a large, white, felt oval on its tummy. The whole thing smelled like mothballs and mold, and there were tiny holes here and there where who-knows-what had nibbled on it. The joints were nearly threadbare. I vaguely remembered Max mentioning that my sewing skills would come in handy with the older costumes. I wish I'd taken the initiative during one or two of my breaks to fix up this thing. Too late now.

Not only had I never seen Billy out of the suit, I had also never seen Billy put on or take off the suit. I had no idea if he had clothes on underneath it. I knew he wore sneakers, but clothes? He must take them off. Otherwise, why would Max have left the room? But isn't it a little creepy to think that the bunny is naked under the suit?

Fuck it, whatever, no time. I took off my clothes, down to my bra and underwear, then pulled on the suit. It was like shrugging into full-body ski pants. It was tight around my thighs and chest—made for a boy, a tiny boy—and where the fabric touched my skin, it itched already. Thank god I had had that depression weight loss recently, or I don't think I would have been able to sit down. The pasta from last night alone made it tough. This was going to be an awful day.

God, I'd never hated Billy more.

"Okay," I said as I slipped on the gloves which, in contrast to the tight suit, were huge and unwieldy, like if oven mitts had individual fingers.

Max came back in to help me with the rest. There were booties to go over my shoes, and then the big head. The head had a strange shape to it—long and tall, with flaps of fabric to cover my neck. The head was taller than my head, and inner netting kept it all in place. The eye holes were actually just at the bottom of the eyes, which were probably why they looked so dead. I peeked in the mirror. With the head on, I was at least half a foot taller than usual. Max took off the head, adjusted the inside like you adjust a bike helmet, and put it back on. It was a little better, but the head still sat high atop my own.

It was dark, behind those tiny mesh eye holes, and it smelled strongly of someone else's sweat. All my senses were dulled, and I was already unbelievably hot. I took off the head again—I had to—and tied my hair at the base of my neck in a tight bun, like a severe school principal. With my hair out of my face and no longer poking into my mouth, the head was a bit better. I gave a loose, half-identifiable thumbs up in those gloves and we were off.

"You know the drill," Max said as we bustled down the service hallway. "Don't talk to the kids—don't talk at all. Make sure both hands are visible, in the photo and at all times. Close your eyes when the photo is taken so your eyes don't glint in the photo. If you're getting overheated or need a break, scratch the bunny ears and I'll try to get you out soon. Otherwise, you're in there for the next four hours."

"I think I can handle it," I said, focusing mainly on not tripping over my own giant feet.

"You'll do great. I'm sure of it."

Every sound was muffled in the suit except my breathing, which was louder than it has ever been before. The head kept shifting down so the eye holes were on my cheekbones and I could only see the floor. I shoved the chin back and up. I could see the second floor of the mall, then the stores, and then it fell down again and I could only see the tile and the heels of Max's shoes. Whatever.

Max barked at me to hurry up, so I did, head lolling, half blind, eyes trained on his shoes as we jog-walked to set.

We must have been within eyesight, because I heard cheers, which quickly fell to confused murmurs—probably because I looked so fucking weird.

"Boys and girls!" Kathi projected. "Look! It's the Easter Bunny!"

I gave a wave. A baby cried. Jesus.

Max led me to the egg-shaped throne and I gently lowered down—but it was lower than I thought and I ended up half falling into it, banging my elbow on one of the sharp edges of the cracked shell. I ground my teeth together to keep from groaning. My head slipped a bit, so all I could see was the front desk and everyone's pants. A little boy laughed, so I played it up, throwing my legs up akimbo and then fake laughing, hands on my tummy, the whole time cursing Billy and wanting to kill myself.

While Kathi gave the explanatory spiel to the family first in line, I adjusted my seat atop the yolk-colored cushion and tried to accept the fact that I would be here for the next four hours. I could tell why Max made *me* do this, not Kathi. It was uncomfortable and horrible already, and there was no way she'd make it to morning break.

He better give me a bonus for this, I thought.

Max was on camera today. Without warning, his pants appeared in my limited eyesight, and then a toddler girl beside him. He scooped her up and placed her on my knee. She nearly slipped off. My legs were too skinny to make a good seat. I placed one of my fat gloves on her shoulder to keep her steady.

Max's shoes headed back to the camera, then suddenly he was back, speaking sweetly to the girl about Easter and surreptitiously adjusting the head of my costume. *Now* I could see the camera.

So that's how Max saved my life.

As Max leaned forward to take the picture, my head slipped back, and then I was looking at the second floor.

I was smiling—dumbly, since you couldn't see my face anyway—and gazing up at the second floor, trying to ask God to smite me down, doing the math on how many kids I would have to sit with before break, and wondering, still, where the hell Billy ran off to, when I saw Ronald. His tattoos had been burned into my brain the first time I saw him, standing on the second floor. There was no mistaking it: Ronald was back, in the same position, another lollipop sticking out his mouth.

And he was pointing a gun at my head.

Twenty-Eight

The Headless Bunnies

I had only just realized what I was seeing when a loud *bang* and a bright light filled the air. I fell back against my set, not feeling pain but certain I had been hit. A dull ache on my forehead throbbed where the bunny head had thwacked against me. The toddler had fallen backward off my knee and was screaming on the ground.

I panicked and ran. The crowd was screaming, running into each other, grabbing their kids, mowing into each other with their strollers, so I ran the opposite direction, behind the chair, away from Ronald.

I chanced a look back—through my jostling eye holes I could see that Ronald was gone from the second floor, but two cronies were running down the escalator, eyes locked on me, guns in each of their hands.

Oh shit shit shit shit shit shit shit.

I swerved left, apparently just in time. A bullet zinged past me to the right and tore into the diamond store, shattering the glass of a display and sending a diamond and crystal peacock to pieces on the floor. I gasped, swore loudly, then *bang,* a bullet hit the pet store window and *it* cracked; another bullet hit the same window and it fell to pieces. The rabbits in the display case make a break for it past the broken glass. I nearly stepped on one but dodged at the last second. I smacked the bunny head off of me with the back of my wrist and it clattered on the tile behind my heels. I took a glance at it as it rolled back. It had a bullet hole in the forehead. Maybe three inches above my own.

Some kid yelled, "The bunny's a girl!" over the pandemonium, and a man with a scary-deep voice shouted, "A girl?!"

I was running on instinct—this was mall hide and seek on hard mode, and I knew I had to get to the spot where I lost Billy. The place where Nora always got the better of me. The intersection. I could go left or right. There was more shouting, screaming, the chittering of the escaped rabbits, and I felt a pull on my gut that someone must have gotten hurt by now. Statistically. They *must* have.

I need to get out. I need to get out.

But I was still a target—a giant, pink target. I needed to get back to my normal clothes. Then I would look like a normal person and could escape more easily. I could grab my car keys and be out of here right away.

I pulled left, darted diagonally, going around the bases the right way this time, and a bullet whizzed past me into MakeAlive Cosmetics. Someone screamed. My ears rang. *Fuck!* Another bullet, another scream, but this one in the opposite direction—my heart clenched.

Did it go into Pandora's Box?

I had no time. I was obviously who they were shooting at. I ducked into the service hallway, looking back at the Easter set as I turned the corner. Parents were mobbing to get out the doors. Two of the men with guns were talking, one of them waving his pistol dismissively. Ronald was gone.

I wrenched open the service hallway door—unmarked except for a small bronze PRIVATE.

I eased the door closed behind me and exhaled. My heart pounded in my ringing ears. *Holy shit.* I turned—and a huge, tattooed figure almost made me scream. Then I realized it was just Billy.

"Billy!" My hand flew over my racing heart in relief, then hardened into a fist. "What the *hell?!* Did you know this was going to happen?"

"No." He reached forward to put a hand on my shoulder, but I leaned back just a bit. He pulled back his hand. "Are you alright?"

"Yeah. The bunny was shot in the forehead, but they missed me."

I gingerly patted the top of my hair, half expecting a burn trail cut from the bullet's path. If I hadn't tied my hair back so tightly, there might have been.

"They want me. They thought you were me," Billy said, gesturing with me to go back out the door. I stayed rooted to the floor.

"Dude, there's a *shooting* going on out there," I said, starting down the service hallway. My hands were shaking so bad. I was talking so fast my words were slurring. "We need to get our car keys and get the fuck out of here."

"They want *me*," Billy repeated. He ran his fingers over his bald head. He was still in the (better) bunny costume, but had ditched the gloves and head as well. Screaming radiated in from outside, then another gunshot, then my dad's voice on a megaphone.

"Shit. Shit! Dad's out there!"

"Shit—Mo, we don't have time to get the keys. We need to get out of here, now."

I pushed away anxious visions of becoming an orphan. "He'll kill us if we go out there."

"You'll be fine, I—ugh!" He pressed the heels of his hands against his temples "Just take off the bunny suit. Then they won't know it's you."

"And running naked through the mall won't tip them off?"

He paused, cinching his eyes closed a bit in disgust. "You're naked under that?"

"I have on underwear."

"…still."

"Oh my *god* dude, not the point! If Ronald sees me, he'll shoot me. He's after *me*," I countered. This finally made Billy freeze and back away from the door. "He talked to my dad," I explained. "He watched me at work. He *shot* at me. You must have been wrong, dude, my mom must have owed him a fortune when she died, and now he's taking it out on me."

Billy pressed his lips together hard, eyes trained on the door handle.

"Mo, I'm sorry. They're not after you. They're after me."

"No, dude, Ronald's going after—"

"*I'm* Ronald."

"…You're—"

"I'm Ronald."

So…that's how I ended up in a mall service hallway during a mass shooting, wearing headless bunny suits with my mom's murderer.

Twenty-Nine

"What do you mean, *you're* Ronald?"

"I changed my name when I moved out here. Your mom wasn't even the first of my clients to overdose, but she was the first with a kid, and that kind of flipped a switch for me. Thinking about you without a mom, because of me…not that I knew you, but Amy talked about you, sometimes. I never thought I'd meet…but god, karma's a bitch."

He looked up, helpless. I shook my head. It was all I could think to do. I think if we weren't in a shooting I would have freaked out. But I was already on high alert and didn't have the time. I knew part of me should have been screaming, but the negative side of my brain was silent, and all I could think in the energy of the moment was, *damn, what a fucking coincidence.*

"I sent those three lunatics to jail for five years. I guess they all got out and tracked me down."

"You gave my mom the drugs that killed her," I said, slowly thinking of Elise, of the people I hurt by stealing without even feeling bad about it. Part of me felt like we should *both* be in jail—for stealing, for hurting others, for second-hand murder. But we weren't. And I didn't want him to be. And maybe that's selfishness, or maybe it's thinking of others, or forgiveness, or something. I didn't have the time to think it through. I just had the time to realize I wasn't as mad at Billy—Ronald—as I thought I would be, and I still wanted to help him, to help the good person I had gotten to know.

So, I just said that fact: "You gave my mom the drugs that killed her," and he nodded, and I nodded, and then I said, "Okay."

"Okay. We need to go," he said.

He knew these people better than I did. I had to trust him.

"Let's go."

But we'd waited too long.

Just as we darted out of the service tunnel, someone yelled, "There!" And Billy ran even faster.

"Go right," I said, and he ducked with me to the right, into the security office. No one was in the office—they must be out there, trying to get everyone safe and stopping the shooters. I was nervous out of my skin, but determined, and I thought that maybe this was me forgiving my mom, and Billy, and myself, and maybe that meant Nora and Elise would one day forgive me, too. Forgiveness—what the "Easter" in "Easter Bunny" was supposed to be about. And funny enough, it was because of Dad—the master of forgiveness—that I knew how to save us, because it was because of Dad that I knew the combination to that locker in the security office. The locker that now belonged to a new recruit.

65, 43, 09. Bang. I swung it open, begging the universe

for something useful. I already knew there wouldn't be a gun, but *something…*

A taser. Holy shit. *Yes.* I grabbed it, flipped it around in fumbling hands, found what I figured to be the safety and switched it off. Did I have to load it? Charge it? Turn it on?

"MO!"

I whirled around on my knees and saw the guy I'd thought was Ronald whip open the door, gun at arm's length, pointed at Billy. I smacked something else on the taser, aimed, and fired.

His gun went off a half second before the taser lodged in his chest, making him groan, seize, and collapse, dropping the gun. A horrible *crack*; confetti burst out of my taser and fluttered through the air like snowflakes. Billy, who was on the floor, probably shot, kicked the dropped gun out of the way.

I fell back against the locker, in shock and half deaf. The taser sparked and sizzled for five long seconds, then died, and the shooter started twitching, slowly moving once again. He pulled himself to his hands and the side of one thigh, coughed, and heaved out bloody bits of lollipop and white chunks of, I think, teeth. He must have bit down on it hard when he got tased.

"You…bitch," the man I once thought was Ronald grunted, and he started crawling toward me, and I backed up on the floor, scared beyond belief, but then Billy threw himself on top of him. I gasped involuntarily, pinning myself up against the wall. Then the two of them were wrestling, both injured but both strong. They rolled over one another, but ended with Billy pinning him, straddling his waist, leaning low over his face for leverage.

The man spit up into Billy's face, bloody and half purple from the lollipop. "Remember me, asshole?"

"Yeah, I remember you," Billy said, almost calmly, keeping the man's shoulders from leaving the ground. "But I'm over it, dude."

The spit dropped off Billy's cheek to land on the man's face again. Well, the other guy didn't like that, and he thrashed against Billy harder. Billy's hand slipped, and the man twisted out of his grasp, knocking Billy to the floor. I swore and turned the taser over in my hands, trying to figure out how to reload or whatever the fuck I had to do with it. Billy managed to get to his knees and tackle the man again—but before he could pin him down, my dad was there, yanking Billy off the man and arresting the shooter, pinning him face-first on the floor, wrenching his arms behind his back. I was surprised my dad could *do* that. I've never seen him that mad.

"You ruined my life!" the guy screamed at Billy from the floor, spit flying out of his mouth. Billy, sitting with his back up against the wall, just breathed heavy at him, not responding. And then two real cops took over for my dad, and then suddenly everyone was hunched over Billy, because it turned out that the guy had shot him in the side, when the gun went off just before he was tased. I was worried, really worried, but then someone said with relief that it probably just grazed his ribs, so he'd be alright. I'm really glad someone said that. I'd still be worried sick if they hadn't. I just hope they were right.

My dad saw me at the other end of the taser wire and practically fell over himself to get to me. We both scrambled to get into a hug on the floor, but I was still kind of in shock, still full of adrenaline. He asked if I was alright, if I was hurt, if I was shot, and I wasn't. I felt the top of my head again to make sure. He asked if I could hear, and I could, but it was still fuzzy. He said the ringing would go away soon. He kissed my forehead and told me to stay put. The other two shooters were already taken care of, but he had to make sure there weren't any more.

"No one else was hurt. Miraculously," he said, standing. Then he paused, got a good look at me, and asked, "Why are you in a bunny suit?"

"Long story. I'll tell you later."

He laughed a little at the absurdity of it all, then he got a buzz on his walkie talkie. One of the employees at the toy store was wigged out over my bag of "returns," so Dad had to run down there to tell them in person that it wasn't related. He said he'd be back soon.

The whole thing lasted six minutes.

I was left in the room with Billy and the cops, who were doing all the first aid at their disposal to stop his bleeding until the ambulances arrived. In retrospect, it was weird that they didn't think he was involved, considering his tattoos— but I guess the giant bunny suit was enough to convince the cops he wasn't exactly dangerous. On top of that, I heard someone say that Billy was the one who called the cops, which was apparently what he did when he ran from me. I don't know why he didn't say anything to me. Panic, I guess.

Or maybe he thought they wouldn't have tried to hurt anyone except him.

But I thought about all that stuff later. Right then, I was just focused on Billy.

I crawled over to him. I wasn't injured or anything, but I was shaking too much to stand.

"Ronald," I said. He looked up at me with his skull eyes.

"I'm sorry," he groaned.

"For what? You're the one who's shot." I laughed, in disbelief. "You saved me, dude! That's infinite good karma! Karma off the charts!"

He smiled, then winced, overtaken by a bout of pain.

"I'll have to move again," he said. The paramedics were here, bringing in a stretcher. God, they moved fast. My heart seized. Suddenly, there was so little time.

"Move again?"

"And change my name again. Maybe they'll finally put me in real witness protection…" He grunted, took a sharp breath. "Now that they found me…Mo, I'll never be able to see you again. For both our safety."

"But…" I looked at every inch of his face, trying to memorize it. I'd never seen him out of his bunny suit, never seen the rest of his tattoos, never met his girlfriend, never heard him play the drums. Soon he'd be getting his face tattoos removed. I couldn't get my mind to visually edit them off his skin. Like his grandmother, I wouldn't recognize him in public. "I hope your girlfriend marries you."

"She'll come with me," he said with a firm nod.

"I hope you find a good place."

"You too. I hope Elise forgives you."

"I hope Ronald's teeth never get fixed."

Billy smirked. "His real name is Tommy. And yeah, I hope they look like a Jack-o'-lantern."

"I…" I felt tears welling up. "I learned a lot from this story."

He smiled a shaky smile. "Yeah. Me too."

Then they were telling me to get out of the way so they could get him on the stretcher. I clutched his hand.

"We never got to play music together," he said, then added, in a disconnected and weirdly casual voice, "Happy Easter."

"Happy Easter."

He squeezed my hand, then let go. And they got him on a stretcher and rushed him out. He and his medical entourage turned the corner, and his bunny ankles and basketball shoes disappeared. And I'll probably never see him again.

"Mo."

Elise. She was a mess, dreadlocks in her face, uniform untucked, standing in the door with her arms by her sides, confused and alone. I staggered to my feet and ran to her, unthinking.

"Are you okay?" I asked, rushing.

"Yes, are you okay?"

"Yes!"

I leaped into her arms and sobbed. She took a few steps back with the momentum, then wrapped her arms tightly around me as I wept, ugly and embarrassing, into her shoulder. I didn't expect to start crying, it just kind of shot out of me. I was so glad she was okay. I was so glad she was holding me, hugging me. She barely knew me. She knew so much about me.

She started crying too. I didn't know or even wonder why. I was done analyzing the reasons and justifications behind emotions—hers and mine, and Nora's, and everyone's. We held each other and fucking cried, and that's all I'm going to dissect about that moment.

"Holy shit, Mo," she said finally and pulled back, makeup running down her face. "Did you really tase somebody?"

My softening sobs turned into laughs, and I nodded, and she said "Holy shit," and I hugged her again. I wasn't sure if that was okay, but her hands on my back pulled me closer, so it must have been. My fingers were shaking, and she felt them shake and then she held them in her hands, pressed them still with her bandaged fingers.

"I'm sorry about the stealing," I said. "I gave back everything I could, and—"

"Mo, we just lived through a shooting, who cares about that?"

"No—it's still important," I insisted, sniffling. Some pet-shop employees ran past, chasing an escaped rabbit. "It's important to you, and me too. And everyone. And I'm sorry I didn't get it before, but I do now. And you were right, I so, *so* regret that I didn't tell you sooner, that I wasn't honest with you. And I promise I'm gonna listen to you, and make things right with Nora and her egged-up house, and—"

And she hugged me again. And then I was laughing.

We were both crying and laughing and shaking and hugging. And all of this was very strange to be happening after a shooting, but I'm done analyzing emotions and things and why they happen. That's your job, not mine.

Thirty

And Then, I Got Arrested

Basically, what the title says.

Long story short, I was hugging Elise, and then suddenly she said, "Oh, shit," then whispered in my ear, "My asshole manager."

We turned and saw a stout woman flanked by cops—real cops, my dad nowhere in sight. And clutched in her hand was a piece of unfolded notebook paper, "Elise" written on the back in my handwriting.

"You wrote this?" one of the cops asked.

I nodded, because what else was I gonna do? And before I knew it, he turned me around, shoved me against the wall, and handcuffed me. Elise backed up in surprise.

"Wait, no," Elise sputtered, eyes locking on mine. "She was—that's not—"

My heart was pounding, but I wasn't nearly as freaked out as I was during the shooting. They led me away, around the corner and to the opposite side of the mall, parading me in my stupid bunny suit past the carnage Tommy and the crew left behind. There were still loose bunnies hopping around the floor, and broken glass, and above it all happy mall music was playing. I glanced back at the Easter Bunny set, at the two escalators beyond it, at the velvet ropes leading to the front desk, at Billy's cracked-egg throne, at the camera I'd lived behind for weeks. And at the head of my costume, discarded, shot through the forehead, smiling on its side twenty feet from the pastel eggshell carpet.

We passed another store with my bag out front—the manager of that store was talking with another cop.

"Please," that cop said, "Just head outside, we'll take care of them."

"I can't have it here if it's gonna—"

"Please, sir—"

"I don't want it blowing up my store, dude, there's half a million in merchandise in—"

"We'll take care of it."

That's when it hit me. They thought my bags were bombs.

So. We've reached the present moment. Well, almost— they got my fingerprints, took my mugshot, and asked me a bunch of questions in a tiny dark room. I did what my dad always said to do and didn't say a word for a while, until they said, "Are you involved with the other people we just arrested? Or are you in with a rival gang?"

"Neither," I said, finally.

"Neither?" Both of the cops exchanged glances, like I was a kid with crumbs on their face lying about eating the last cookie. "Then, what's up with the bomb scare? Trying to get people out of the mall? Terrorize them a bit? Ruin those guys' plan, right?"

I told them I had no idea about their plan. I pointed

out that I was shot at—if I knew about their plan, would I have even gone to work that day? I asked if they opened the bags, and they said they did, and just found clothes, trinkets, etc.

I *almost* opened my big mouth and told them what all that stuff really was, but Dad's advice to shut up came back to me and I just left it there. It was clothes, not bombs, and I had no idea about the other guys' plans. Eventually, that was enough for them to bring me to the holding cell.

I was alone in the cell, except outside the cell one cop was on guard, doing paperwork. I asked for a pen and paper, and I guess she felt bad for me, in my stupid itchy bunny suit, because she gave me some. A whole notebook, actually. So as the hours went on, I wrote to you. Because I don't know what's going to happen, and I don't know if my dad or I will be able to convince everybody that I wasn't involved, especially after working with Billy for so long, and the connection—assuming they find out about the connection—between his gang and my mother. Probably they'll decide even if the bags weren't bombs that they were supposed to look like bombs, and put me in jail for a million years.

I can hear my dad outside. So, I guess this is it. I hope you get this, and you know how much you helped me. Whatever happens, it will be better than it would have

Epilogue

How to Act Normal on Easter Morning

Ready to hear how dad got me out of jail and got me a new job, all at once?

He showed up and I left the notebook on the floor, running to the bars. He took my hand, heart breaking in his eyes.

"Sorry this happened," he whispered, "but you're getting out of here. Just stay quiet until we get outside."

Right behind him were two of the cops that had been at the mall. Dad shook hands with one of them while the other unlocked the cell. I wandered out, a bit numb.

"You'll let us know if you have any other questions?" Dad asked.

The cop nodded. "Yeah. We might need both of you as a witness. But thank you for clearing the bag business up."

"Happy to do it."

The cop who opened the cell gestured to the notebook on the floor. "That yours?"

Right. I scooped it up, gave the pen back to the cop at the desk, and followed at my dad's heels out of the station.

"What happened?" I asked in a low voice when we got outside. It was dark out. They'd given me a sandwich and a bottle of water at some point, but I was starving.

"Shh. Wait till we get in the car."

We buckled in, and country music flooded the car as he pulled out of the station. I held my notebook filled with these letters to my chest. The bunny suit was small, itchy, and cold. I wished he brought me clothes to change into.

"So!" Dad said, trying to cheer me up. He turned down the radio so it was nearly inaudible again as he turned onto the main road. The sun was setting now. "We've been developing loss-prevention training classes for the stores at the mall. You know, to teach the managers and employees how to spot and stop a thief."

It took a minute for my brain to process anything unrelated to what had just happened. After a second, I managed to reply, "Good. They need it."

That got a laugh out of him. "Yeah, apparently. Anyway, I'm thinking—since the Easter thing is over, maybe you could help us out with that. Help each store identify weak spots. In other words—shoplift, on my orders. I saw on TV once, something called 'White Hat Hacking.' Well, this would be white hat shoplifting. It will show the managers just how much the training is needed. And you can show them all how you did it!"

"I…"

"In fact, let's say you start at this new job a week ago. And that this whole thing was a big misunderstanding—my fault, my attempt at making a point, unfortunately and coincidentally happening on the same day as an unconnected shooting." He glanced over at me, his eyes asking, *Catch my drift?*

"So that's what you told them?" I thought over what he said, and it sounded pretty smart. "And it worked?"

"It worked. There's a few more things we have to do—like get you on payroll, and talk to all the managers, and, god, maybe buy Max a weighted blanket so he stops shaking. It's not all over yet, but I wasn't having my baby go to jail for gang-involved bombing when I knew all she did was shoplift and get shot at."

"You lied to them?" I said, not sure which word to stress most.

"It was the right thing to do."

Slowly, I looked back out the windshield. Elise was right. The world really isn't black and white.

So I guess my new job will be, believe it or not, shoplifting. When it finally sunk in, it actually sounded pretty fun. Like a secret health inspector, but cool. I'd still get to put my skills to use, but for the good of the mall.

For the good of the big businesses who don't need the—

No. For the good of the employees, like Elise. I can get back at capitalism some other way.

When I got home, I was like a wild animal. I tore off the bunny suit and leapt in the shower, showered quick as I could, then scarfed down a huge dinner and practically collapsed in my bed. Dad had given me my phone back, and before I fell asleep, I ran through and gave everyone an "I'm okay" message.

Claire and John both heard about it from a friend of a

friend. I told them I was fine and would explain more tomorrow.

Elise had sent me a message or two every hour. I spent more time on her, because after I said *I'm okay, I'm home,* she sent me a flutter of messages about how she wanted to see me right now. It took a while to tell her I was too tired but I would see her tomorrow without it seeming like I was blowing her off. But eventually she agreed, ending with, *I'm so, so, so glad you're okay.*

Then there was Nora. We hadn't talked in ages. But she had sent me a text: *Claire said you're in jail? And were in a shooting? Are you okay?*

I'm okay, I wrote back. *Thanks.*

Good, thank god, she replied soon after.

I stared at the message for a long time. *I'm figuring out some stuff,* I finally wrote back. *But can you and I hang out soon? Talk about stuff?*

I actually fell asleep before she replied, but when I woke up, I saw she'd said, *Okay, sure.*

The next morning was Easter. We don't go to church every Sunday or anything, but my grandmother likes us to go on the holidays, so we do. Dad and I got up early to eat some hard-boiled eggs before heading out. I had initially planned to color them the night before Easter, before everything happened. Oh well. I ate three, and I could tell he was surprised, but he didn't mention it. I was also surprised. I was worried that, you know, being in a shooting and getting arrested would worsen my lack of appetite, but it didn't seem to. So maybe I only have four out of seven signs of depression, now. Or maybe overeating is a sign of trauma? Jeez. You can't win.

Dad probably wanted me to wear something ladylike and pastel to church, but I wore a dark suit and tie, and he didn't say anything about it. I sat in the pew between my dad and my grandmother. My eyes stung. My dad squeezed my hand.

I felt emotionally hungover. I was kind of still shaking. I imagined Elise's bandaged fingers pressing mine still, and that helped a little.

The priest was talking about the meaning of Easter and whatever, and I kind of sighed to myself in the pew. I was the *master* of the meaning of Easter, dude. Easter's about eggs, chocolate, and the bunny at the mall. It's also about forgiveness, like how Jesus forgave the people who killed him. It's also about celebrating the fact that Jesus, who you thought was dead, came back to life for...a week?

No one really talks about what Jesus did *after* he came back. Everyone's too psyched over the fact that he came back at all. But why? Did anyone in the church wonder *why* it was so great that he came back, if the point was that he *died* for our sins? Did the sacrifice matter if he came back— and hell, if he's immortal, anyway? It's not like he's still walking around to this day, turning water into wine, so why was everyone so happy?

I ran my eyes over the wooden carving of dead Jesus and reminded myself that no one needs to justify how they feel. Not even me. So if Easter made these people happy, that's great. I think it will always make me sad, from now on, because I'll always be thinking of Billy, the complicated, wonderful friend I'll never see again. It'll remind me of Tommy, the terrifying lollipop guy who went to prison because Billy sold him out; the guy who got bit in the ass by his own revenge scheme and who might have avoided all of it had he made different choices. It'll remind me of Ronald, the badass who came back from the dead to keep Tommy from attacking me, and the nameless, tattooless person who used to be Billy and who used to be Ronald, but who will soon be running around with a new name and a reborn, inkless face that a grandmother, somewhere, might recognize again. I'll also be thinking about the time I was wearing a bunny suit that got shot between the eyes, which will probably cause all kinds of awesome psychological problems later on. Can't wait for *that*. Good thing I already have you. And good thing you agreed to letting me come twice a week now.

The first step was figuring out what I'm feeling and accepting it. I'm not perfect, but I'm doing better at that all the time. I think the *next* step is learning how to act on my feelings. To know what they are and to know what to do about them. How to manage them and how to express them in all their nuance.

So, I guess that's where I need your help next.

Doctor, I miss Billy already. I still miss Mom. I don't know how to apologize to Nora, and I have no idea what to say to Elise, or if we're together again, or not, or what to do with her at all. I'm worried, still, that my dad secretly thinks I'm a thieving failure, and I'm worried that Billy isn't going to be okay.

And maybe all these emotions are unjustified, but it's how I feel. And I realize now that however I feel is okay.

Acknowledgements

No writer is an island, and I am certainly no exception. I could thank every person I've ever met, and it would not be inaccurate, as everybody the writer meets affects the writer's work—but doing so individually would take more pages than the book itself. Thank you, my family, my friends, my teachers, and so on. If I know you, thank you. Know that you're listed in my heart, if not on paper.

That said, I'd like to highlight a few people who helped me along this specific journey.

Thank you everyone at Deep Hearts YA for taking a chance on me and my debut novel. You have been wonderful every step of the way, and have made my first book publishing experience an amazing one. The work you are doing to highlight queer voices and stories like this one is phenomenal.

Thank you to my writing circle—Logan Chamberlain, Darian Clogston, Drew Harris, Jack Marrinson, and Annette Sherrod. Without you, this book would never have gotten to where it is today. Thanks also to my beta readers and early editors—Colin, Ellison, Qatarina Wanders, and Steve Kordell—who provided the insight I needed right when I needed it.

Thanks, Wandering Words Media, for giving me a dream job that teaches me continually about my craft.

Thanks, Billerica Memorial High School, Emerson College, and all my teachers of every kind.

Thanks, Shawsheen Valley Technically High School, for teaching me that I wanted to spend my time inspiring and helping teenagers and young adults. Thanks to all the kids I worked with, there—spending time with you and seeing your bravery, wisdom, humor, kindness, and perseverance in the face of struggle helps me write decently realistic teenagers today.

Finally, thank you, for keeping at it.

About the Author

Christina Bagni is the chief editor at Wandering Words Media and a writer on the Captain Bitcoin comic book series. She loves mythology, rock climbing, buying far too many books to ever actually read, and writing the kind of queer-led stories she wished she had as a teenager. My Only Real Friend is the Easter Bunny at the Mall is her first novel. She lives in Massachusetts.

Find more about her at linktr.ee/christinabagni

More From Deep Hearts YA

Mark of Ravage and Ruin

Jacyn Gormish

Trapped in the Asylum and destined to become an assassin, Barli wants nothing more than to escape and return to the arms of her girlfriend. But when the moment arises for possible freedom, she learns that a friend is to be killed—and only Barli can save him.

Gerald Ribbon and the Bird in His Brain

Maxwell Bauman

Gerald Ribbon has a habit of ruining his love life, and the bird in his brain that gives him terrible advice certainly isn't helping.

The Mixtape to My Life

Jake Martinez

Justin has always been comfortable in his skin, even if the world around him wasn't. A junior simply counting down the days for when he can leave for college, Justin's life is thrown for a loop when the one thing that helps him feel like himself suddenly slips away from him. But an unexpected blast from his past puts summer on a new and exciting path, one as random and unexpected as a mixtape.

More From Deep Hearts YA

Invisi Gir1
Conner Steel

Emma is trying to leave her previous life as a hacker behind, but when she meets Halo Ironside, it soon becomes clear he's baiting her to dive back into her old persona of Invisi_Gir1.

Fairy War
E.J. Graham

When Clint narrowly escapes an attack on his family home, he discovers that the world is far more magical—and dangerous—than he could have possibly imagined.

Geist
Mark Kelly

The Geist exist to ferry ghosts away from dead bodies and into the gates of the afterlife. At least, that's what Ash Murphy was told after he died in a fiery car crash and became one.

Deep Hearts YA publishes
LGBTQ+ young adult fiction.

Please follow us on social media or visit our website to find out more.

Instagram: instagram.com/DeepHeartsYA
Twitter: twitter.com/DeepHeartsYA
Facebook: facebook.com/DeepHeartsYA
Website: deepheartsya.com

www.ingramcontent.com/pod-product-compliance
Lightning Source LLC
Chambersburg PA
CBHW030816210726
48290CB00002B/619